THE WORLD MAKER
PARABLE

THE WORLD MAKER PARABLE

AN ADJACENT MONSTERS NIGHTMARE

LUKE TARZIAN

ALSO BY LUKE TARZIAN

THE SHADOW TWINS SERIES

Vultures

House of Muir (Forthcoming)

ANTHOLOGIES

Dark Ends

For Celia and Naomi...
Daddy loves you

JÉMOON

HANG-DEAD FOREST

BANEROWOS

THE SONJA OCEAN

"Midway upon the journey of our life, I found myself within a forest dark, for the straightforward pathway had been lost."

— Dante Alighieri, *The Inferno*

1

PENDULUM DANCE

Hᴀɴɢ-Dᴇᴀᴅ Fᴏʀᴇsᴛ ɴᴏʀᴛʜ of Banerowos was aptly named. Rhona had lost count of the corpses half a mile back. She towed her prisoner on a length of cord. Thus far she had ignored Djen's every word, half because she was tired of listening to the woman spit hatred, and half because Rhona wasn't entirely sure how to respond. Leading the woman you loved to the tree from which she was sentenced to hang had that effect.

"I do as the Raven wills," Rhona said.

Djen spat. "Fuck Alerion. Fuck *you* and your reflexive bullshit."

They ducked beneath a trio of low-hanging corpses. The dark bones were long picked dry. Only tatters of clothing remained.

"It's the truth," said Rhona. "Alerion's will is our

command. Those who ignore him are a threat to the continued unification of home."

"You really *are* full of shit," Djen hissed. "Alerion's words are so ingrained into your skull they may as well be his hand shoved up your ass and moving your mouth." She heaved a sigh. "Never in all my years would I have thought you'd be the one to dance on strings. I suppose I never really knew you at all, Rhona."

Rhona halted. She had tried these last hours, these last days, to ignore the bitterness Djen spat her way. Some of it was rightly earned—Rhona didn't deny that. She just wished Djen could understand *why* she had done what she had done.

"I suppose if I had," Djen continued, "I would have foreseen you betraying me to Alerion."

"How could I *not?*" Rhona asked. "You *unleashed* the Vulture from her cage."

"I *had* to, you idiot," Djen snarled. "You and Alerion all but doomed us when you imprisoned Luminil. What I did was for the future of our home. For the survival of this country and its people. If you would open your eyes—if you would *all* open your eyes—you would see how absolutely wrong you were to have kept such power in chains."

Rhona yanked the cord and they continued on the way. She focused on the forest; she had always found peace here among the dead. For that, some called her mad, but what did she care? She inhaled deeply. The trees smelled of death and fear, if fear could be said to smell like anything at all. To

Rhona, fear smelled like a foul breath clouding in the night, and that too was a very particular scent. In Hang-Dead Forest a foul breath was defined as an odor of iron and rain—magic. Mirkúr.

They marched on through gnarled and twisted trees. Guilt nipped at Rhona's heels like a hungry dog and her heart stung. It wasn't supposed to have come to this. She loved Djen for all her flaws, for the gravity of her sin—could she really string her up to rot amongst the dead? Could she really watch Djen join the countless corpses in their pendulum dance?

"You'll have to whether you like it or not," her conscience said. It called itself Fiel. "Country over person—it is the Raven's way. Alerion's will is our command." It sighed. "How could we have ever loved such a thing as Djen Shy'eth?"

Rhona frowned. *Ever the formal voice of woe,* she thought. Fiel—the vocal trauma to her silent grief. Loving Djen had come easily to Rhona. In fact, it had been the easiest thing she had ever done, which made it all the more nauseating how quickly she had turned Djen over to Alerion. Had Rhona always been so fickle?

"No," Fiel said. "You are doing what you know is right. Country over person. If minds like those of Djen Shy'eth and Sonja Lúm-talé can be so easily swayed by the darkness of the Vulture Luminíl then what reason do you have to believe a word they say? The Vulture is the personification of entropy—Luminíl had to be contained."

3

They came to a small clearing in the depths of the forest. At the center was a tree unique from all the others: white of bark and black of leaves. For that Rhona called it the Lost Tree; it seemed so out of place in a wooded world of death and fog.

Yet by branches have so many lives been claimed, she thought. From the branches of the Lost Tree she would hang her beloved Djen; to its roots Rhona would give her own blood in reverence. Blood paid was a debt owed and it was best to curry favor where you could, especially in times like this where uncertainty was king.

"If you would stop taking sips from the wine Alerion serves," Djen said, "you would know how absolutely wrong he was, how wrong you are. You would understand the severity of what you did to Luminíl." She sighed as they stopped at the base of the Lost Tree. "You will..."

Rhona turned to look at Djen. It was the first time she had done so since leaving Banerowos. For a moment she allowed herself to get lost in Djen's full-moon eyes, to imagine the taste of her lips and the gentle warmth of her breath.

"Keep your tongue," said Djen. "You have that look, but your words mean nothing."

Rhona flinched and it pulled her from her dream. She dropped Djen to her knees and drew a dagger from her cloak. "I wish things could be different."

Djen smirked. "No you don't—but you will. Get on with it."

"Alf elo nor," Rhona chanted. *"Nor elo alf!"*

She punched the blade into Djen.

Then she did the same to herself.

––––––

"ONCE MORE YOU RETURN."

Rhona opened her eyes to the ethereal voice she had heard so many times before. Before her towered a lithe figure of smoke and wings. It called itself Equilibrium. It offered a hand and pulled her to her feet.

"It has been a while since last we spoke," said Equilibrium.

"It has," Rhona said. She gazed into the vast whiteness that encompassed them, feeling peace where others had undoubtedly felt dread. The Silent Place was many things to many different souls. She heaved a sigh.

"You have questions," Equilibrium said. "As you always do." The spirit brushed a hand against her cheek and she felt a modicum of weightlessness. "What brings you to the Silent Place this night?"

Rhona did her best to breathe evenly, composing her thoughts as best she could. She wanted everything to be presented as clearly as it could be. With her left index finger she traced the air, leaving gossamer symbols in her wake. Equilibrium reached out with its right index finger and traced them in reverse.

"So much conflict," the spirit murmured. "So much heartache."

The whiteness of the Silent Place dissolved in rivulets. In its place a meadow manifested. A sea of silver grass beneath a moon like none that Rhona had ever seen. Several yards away stood a tree. *The* tree. The Lost Tree. Equilibrium led her at an even pace, its great wings trailing into the ether.

"This is new," Rhona remarked. The Silent Place had never before been more than a brilliant void of nothingness. "Have my memories done something?"

"You are the first to whom the truest nature of the Silent Place has manifested," Equilibrium said. "This is a realm of memory and thought, a means for introspection, for retrospection, however they may be achieved. It is a haven for the dreaming dead."

Rhona brushed the trunk of the Lost Tree. She felt a tingle in her chest—but of what?

"Was I wrong?" she asked. "Has my life these many years been nothing but a lie?"

"You present your question broadly but you focus solely on the woman Djen Shy'eth," Equilibrium said. "What do *you* think, Rhona? What does your mind tell you that your heart does not, that it refuses to?"

"Only that I am conflicted," Rhona said. She felt stupid for her answer, for the ignorance and simplicity of her words. "I loved Djen, but I love Jémoon—I love my home. *Our* home. What Djen did threatened the livelihood of all I hold dear..."

"But?" Equilibrium asked.

"But...but..." Rhona wrinkled her nose. "*I* pushed her to recklessness. *I* pushed her to unleash the Vulture Luminíl—but why? Why would she do something like that? And what did *I* do to push her away?" She looked up at Equilibrium. The spirit gazed back from the darkness of its cowl. "I'm confused by it all."

"Condemning loved ones to their ends has that effect on everyone who swings the sword," said Equilibrium. "The guilt and retrospection manifest far quicker in some than in others. In you, long before Djen's end. The heart often acts on impulse; it is fueled by desire strong enough to suppress logic either temporarily or permanently. What did you desire most, Rhona? What did your heart scream for?"

She opened her mouth to speak but the meadow had already begun to fade. Like the whiteness before it, the meadow dripped away in rivulets until the Silent Place was an endless void as black as the abyss.

Then, she saw a light.

———

THE GRAY of Hang-Dead Forest was soothing to Rhona's eyes. The smell of rain and death upon the breeze eased her mind as she strung Djen's corpse to the lowest branch of the Lost Tree. As Rhona worked the memory of her time in the

Silent Place returned and she found herself asking repeatedly the question Equilibrium had posed:

"What did my heart scream for?"

"A great many things," Fiel remarked. *"A great many things, amongst them Djen Shy'eth."*

Something more than Djen, Rhona thought. *Something strong enough to push her away.*

"Power has the tendency to do that," said Fiel.

Rhona frowned, turning away from the tree. *What are you saying?*

"What, for the longest time, you sought yet at the same time denied you did," Fiel said. *"Control. Authority."*

That's madness, Rhona thought.

"Is it?"

Rhona was silent. Her body ached, her mind howled with the pain of uncertainty. She turned to Djen and brushed her cold cheek. She looked her in the eyes and in them saw a thousand possibilities evanesce. The future was forever fickle. Did that mean Rhona was as well?

She pressed her lips to Djen's one final time.

Then she walked away, waiting for the words that Djen would never say.

2

OPEN WATER

Then

"I LOVE YOU," Djen said, and Rhona nearly toppled over the balustrade.

Rhona steadied herself and looked Djen in her brilliant, stark white eyes. Had she heard her properly? Had Djen said what Rhona had been dying to say? She took a deep breath then exhaled as smoothly as she could so as not to betray her nerves.

"And I love you," Rhona said. Whispered, really. She was trembling. The moonlight shone upon them, upon the distant lake, unobstructed for the first night in weeks; it made Rhona feel warm. She focused on that warmth as she once more tried to compose herself lest Djen think her words were false.

Djen took Rhona's hands in hers. Her trembling subsided almost as quickly as it had come and for that she was grateful. For Djen, she was immensely grateful. They stood in the silent night, the winter chaos of Banerowos's streets little more than a dull buzz below.

"I've dreamt of this for so long," Rhona said, caressing Djen's knuckles with her thumbs. "Of standing here with you, everything else little more than an afterthought." Her cheeks were hot. "Djen..."

Djen smiled. "Me too."

She pulled Rhona toward her. Their faces were just inches apart. Rhona could feel the warmth of Djen's breath and it smelled like mint. Her hair smelled of vanilla and... Rhona shuddered at the pure intoxication of her scent. She wrapped her arms around the woman's waist and pressed her lips to Djen's. A spark rippled through her body—this felt right. This *was* right.

"I've been wanting to do that for...I don't know how long," Rhona murmured when they finally pulled apart. "Years. Decades, even."

"Me too," Djen whispered. She turned, resting her elbows against the balustrade. "I've never seen the lake so bright before, at least not that I can remember."

"I saw it once," Rhona said, mimicking Djen's posture. "Long ago when Banerowos was little more than a skeleton of its current self. You were speaking to Alerion about something. I don't recall what, but it must have been important to you. You jabbed him in the chest with your finger and whatever he had been so eager about vanished from his face."

"Mmm. I remember that," Djen mused softly. "Don't remember what we were arguing about but I most certainly won."

"And Alerion's been calmer ever since," said Rhona. "Silly winged man."

"Careful now," Djen said. "Gods aren't fond of such talk."

Rhona rolled her eyes. "Luckily Alerion seems to have developed an aptitude for discerning sarcasm and fun."

"You have a point. Humility is an appealing characteristic for a god to possess."

"I spoke with the Vulture today," Rhona said. The abruptness of her statement drew a gasp from Djen. "Calm, now. You'd think I told you I murdered someone. I met her in the Raven's Wood for meditation."

Djen offered a slight frown.

"What?"

"Just...be careful around her," Djen said. "She can be volatile."

"As can the Phoenix," said Rhona, "but only if provoked."

"I suppose," Djen said. "Thankfully we've Alerion to keep them both in check."

"Exactly," Rhona said, leaning into Djen. "Besides, they helped to form what we call home. Without that winged trio of creation Banerowos would be little more than a dream. *Jémoon* would be little more than a dream. A fantasy."

Djen sighed. "I suppose you have a point. It's just...such power makes me wary. I'm not the only one. The three of them could destroy us with the snap of a finger. We're little more than playthings for gods if you really think about it, Rhona."

"I *have* thought about it," Rhona said. "Sometimes the notion makes me feel smaller than a speck of dust. But mostly...it makes me feel safe, if that makes any sense. It makes me feel important such primordial beings would see us as their equals in a way. They walk amongst us willingly. That counts for something."

"It does," agreed Djen.

Again, they stood in silence.

"It's enchanting," Djen said.

"Hmm?"

"Each ripple on the surface of the lake," Djen said. "A thousand possibilities manifest and evanesce repeatedly."

Rhona had never thought about it like that. "How many ripples do you think were involved in our creation? In that of Jémoon and Banerowos?"

"Impossible to say," Djen said. "To comprehend, really."

"Probably best not to lest we drive ourselves insane," Rhona said.

"Probably."

Djen draped an arm around Rhona's shoulders. They stood and they stared.

———

Luminíl was beautiful in the same way death inevitable. She was entropy where the Phoenix Mirkvahíl was creation. She was destruction for the greater good, for the evolution of their world, and her power was such that Rhona couldn't help but feel small in her presence despite being half a head taller.

Luminíl stood at the base of a great tree in the center of the Raven's Wood. Where the others bore leaves of red and green, this one's leaves were black and its trunk was whiter than virgin snow.

"I have been waiting for you, Rhona," Luminíl said. Her voice was a gentle breeze.

Rhona approached at a measured pace. She felt little reason to be afraid, anxious—but there was *still* reason. She stopped several feet shy of where the Vulture stood and bowed her head.

"You need not be so formal," Luminíl said. "Long have we known each other, after all."

"Of course," Rhona said. "What's on your mind?"

Luminíl turned to her. It was all Rhona could do to stifle a gasp. Dark veins webbed outward from her once-white, now-red eyes. Rhona had never seen Luminíl so...so...

"Something is wrong with me," the Vulture said. "I am ill

and have been for some time."

"How?" Rhona asked. "What's happening to you?"

"I do not know," Luminíl said. It was the first time Rhona had ever heard fear in her voice. "It started in my dreams and has since manifested itself physically."

Luminíl had never mentioned her dreams to Rhona.

"Have you told Mirkvahíl or Alerion?" Rhona asked.

"I fear their reactions."

Rhona frowned. "But why? You are each one third of creation. And Mirkvahíl is your beloved. What harm could they do?"

Luminíl extended a hand. "I could show you. I could show you everything, Rhona."

A flurry of emotions swam through Rhona, curiosity and fear the strongest of them all. She had been invited to peek into the mind of a goddess—how many people could claim that? But how would she react to Luminíl's dreams? What would the Vulture's dreams do to Rhona? What would *Luminíl* do to Rhona?

"Well?" Luminíl took a step toward her.

Rhona extended a trembling hand. "This won't hurt, will it?"

"I cannot say for certain," Luminíl said. "I will keep you as safe as I am able."

The Vulture's words inspired little confidence, but she was Rhona's friend and you were supposed to help friends in need, were you not? She took Luminíl's hand.

"What now?"

"Be still," Luminíl said. The Raven's Wood swirled and dripped away in rivulets. "Be still."

Now

Rhona hadn't thought about that night in the Raven's Wood in years. Probably for as long as the Raven's Wood had been Hang-Dead Forest. It had changed her, molded her. For better or for worse, she wasn't sure. On one hand she hated what she'd seen in Luminíl's dreams, hated what her exposure to them had done. It had cost Rhona her friendship with Luminíl. It had cost her Djen. But it had saved Banerowos, had saved the whole of Jémoon, and wasn't that the most important thing?

"Is that what you truly believe?" Fiel asked.

What do you mean?

"You tell yourself what you saw in the Vulture's dreams was the catalyst for everything," Fiel said. "Is that really true, or it something you tell yourself to mask a horrible reality?"

What would I be denying? Rhona asked.

"That you were always wary of the Vulture," Fiel said. "That she tricked you into revealing your true nature—your desire for control, for authority over those who scare you most.

Like Luminíl herself. Like Djen Shy'eth and Sonja Lúm-talé."

That's ridiculous, Rhona spat. *In those dreams I saw the end of everything. What I did* saved *Jémoon. I saved* Luminíl, *whether she and her acolytes care to admit so or not. If not for Alerion, Mirkvahíl, and myself this world would be dead.*

Fiel chuckled. *"You say that, yet here we are having this conversation. Here* you *are, thinking to yourself you ought to have a conversation with Alerion, or Varésh Lúm-talé perhaps."*

Rhona growled. She continued through Hang-Dead Forest; Banerowos was still a way off, probably an hour or so. There was a grain of truth to what Fiel said. Life was like open water, each wave, each ripple ripe with possibility.

What do you suppose I should do? Rhona asked Fiel.

"Whatever your gut suggests," Fiel said. *"One's gut instinct is more often than not correct, especially relative to the heart and mind. Do whatever you must to see the truth in all this madness."*

Madness. There was a lot of that going around these days thanks in no small part to Djen and Sonja. How had they been so weak of will? How could they have let Luminíl influence their actions? Alerion might have insight, as might Varésh. But there was someone Rhona felt would be more reliable.

She was going to request an audience with the Phoenix Mirkvahíl.

3

FLIGHTLESS BIRD

VARÉSH LÚM-TALÉ WAS A FAILURE. He had always been the least skilled Architect; the other Celestials thought it an affront he had risen to such prominence. The title of Architect and the responsibilities that came with such a rank were reserved for the most respected of the Celestials and Varésh knew he was on the opposite end of the spectrum. It didn't help matters he had been appointed to his current position by Ouran, the Celestial Emperor. It helped even less Varésh was the favored son of Ouran. He had yet to figure out why.

"*Yet here you are, having wrought this world,*" his conscience said. "*Here you are, the false king of Harthe.*" A Celestial word meaning Harmony. Another lie, the grandest of them all, Varésh had come to learn.

"What say you, O Crown of Harmony?" his conscience sneered.

Varésh walked in silence as the voice berated him. Before him sat a vast expanse of grass, a sea of gold, soft and gentle like the feathers of the Phoenix Mirkvahíl whom Varésh sought. He sought a great many things, redemption most of all, and Mirkvahíl was the grandest requisite.

"You assume the Phoenix lives," his conscience remarked as he waded through the tall reeds. The clouds shifted white to gray to gold and back. *"You assume you can so easily negate your idiocy and that, dear boy, is your arrogance shining brighter than the sun."*

"Do you have a better idea?" Varésh asked aloud. "This entire journey all you've done is whine. All you've done is chide and ridicule and hiss."

His conscience snorted. *"After everything you have done, Varésh Lúm-talé, after everything you have subjected me to, I think I have earned that right* at least. *Would you care to disagree? No—do not answer. My query was rhetorical."*

Varésh kept on at a measured pace. He had been at this for weeks, following the telltale signs of Mirkvahíl's rebirth. Life where once there had been death. Brilliance where once the light was silent. But most of all, the dreams. The images and whispers born of illum prying memories from the depths of the abyss.

"How naive I was and am and always will be 'til the end of time." One needn't cross the Temporal Sea to see that

Varésh would forevermore be prone to idiocy. It was evident in his actions and his words.

"*The irony,*" his conscience mused. "*As if Mirkvahíl could help you rectify your wrongs. As if this plan of yours will sidestep the ruin yet to come. Why do you think your father bequeathed this planet unto you? Have you ever sat and thought? Have you ever walked the tomb of memory in search of clarity?*"

Varésh had not—until recently, at least. Introspection had always made him wary for the simple fact he had always been afraid to learn the hidden truths about himself and otherwise. It had taken holocaust to finally acknowledge what he had been, was, and always would be.

"*Failure,*" his conscience prodded. "*It rings in your ears. It buzzes like a thousand flies above a corpse. It is your legacy, Varésh Lúm-talé, and what a miserable thing it is. What a miserable thing she is.*"

Varésh shivered. She. The Vulture Luminíl. Entropy unbounded. Chaos freed by arrogance and lust and lies.

"*How many lives? How many, do you think?*" The question rang in Varésh's ears, high-pitched and unrelenting. "*Thousands? Hundreds of thousands? Millions, even? What would your beloved Sonja think could she see what you have done, could she see the monster you have made?*"

His conscience manifested at his side, hawk-faced with eyes of light and shadow and a mane of midnight hair. "*What* would Sonja think could she see what you've become, could she see what you have done?"

Varésh trembled at the question, shook with misery and rage. "You keep her name from this."

"Just as you kept her life?" his conscience sneered. "Your Sonja deserved more than you were, Varésh Lúm-talé. She deserved more than you ever will be. She saw from the start what you needed a catastrophe to see. They all saw and for that they are dead."

Varésh tensed his jaw. "Mirkvahíl will help me make this right."

"He said naively," mocked his conscience. "You place your faith in the idea of Mirkvahíl as blindly as your people bow to your father's every whim—and look where that has led!"

Varésh stared across the vastness of this place. He could feel it in the pit of his stomach, his absolute fear, the desperation of his endeavor.

"If you were strong you would strike your father down," his conscience said. "You would sever ties, free your people from his madness and his lust for universal conquest. You would have them be true Architects, true World Builders, not the lies Ouran has made them.

"But you are not strong. You are desperate and you are ignorant, and so you go about this task of yours. You seek to rectify a wrong you cannot undo and it will haunt you 'til the end of days whenever that may be."

The manifestation vanished. Varésh was alone with the

grass and the clouds, with the wind and his thoughts. *It* will *work,* he urged himself. *It* has *to.* If not the personification of preservation and renewal, what could quell the destructive nature of the Vulture Luminíl?

"How could I have ever let it come to this?" lamented Varésh. A great ruin of ice and stone flashed across his mind. A dark world. A dead world. It filled him with more shame and guilt and disgust. He hated himself, and he hated that he hated himself. But that was part of the experience, he supposed. The experience of introspection in the wake of failure. The experience *of* failure.

And maybe that was why his undertaking had a chance to succeed. Success bloomed from the seeds sown by failure, or so he had taken to telling himself. His idiocy was a parable from which greater things could come if he made sure not to make the same mistakes again. If he was going to be an Architect, a World Builder in the truest form of the term, that meant giving a shit.

He walked.

Raindrops fell.

———

VARÉSH HAD SEEN MUCH of Harthe in these last years. As planets went it was an infinitesimal thing, large yet scarcely populated. In his youth he had fantasized about the day he might be made an Architect, be made to shape and mold worlds, to nurture them from infancy to maturation. The notion of parenthood had always appealed to Varésh—what could be grander than fatherhood in the context of rearing an entire world?

"Do you truly believe you can set things right?" he asked of himself as the wandered through the rain. "How does a parent come back from *that*, from ignorance? From annihilation born of arrogance?"

"*And a false sense of unity,*" his conscience said.

"Of course..."

Varésh stopped. He was soaked to the bone but he did not care. He stood and stared, trained his ears to a faint but anguished melody behind the liquid misery and clouds. He had heard it so many times these last years, increasingly these last few weeks.

"Mirkvahíl," he whispered. The louder her song grew, the nearer Varésh knew he was.

"*Or perhaps you are imagining it,*" his conscience said, "*as you imagined so many things before. A man who fancies himself a god is the biggest lie of all, and all he does comes from a false heart.*"

Varésh choked back tears. He *had* fancied himself a god in his yesteryears—things were the way they were because of that. But he had changed. Celestials, he had *changed*! Why else would Mirkvahíl have called to him? Why would the Phoenix call to a man not pure of heart?

"*What makes you think your heart is pure? What makes*

you think your motivation comes from a place of remorse? Truths are lies we tell ourselves," his conscience hissed. "Lies we tell ourselves to mask the monsters that we really are. The truth, Varésh Lúm-talé, is not so easily discerned from madness. In fact, they are more often than not one and the same."

His shadow twin manifested and caressed his cheek with a wispy hand. "Which one of us is real, Varésh?"

Varésh trembled at its touch. Its words chilled his blood.

"What makes you think me your conscience, hmm? From where, pray tell, did that little notion arise? His shadow twin grinned as its shape waned. Think on it as you walk, but remember this: I am not suck in here with you...

"You are trapped in here with me."

Varésh retched at its lingering touch. Retched as he never had before. He crumpled to the grass and curled himself into a ball, hugging his knees to his chest. It could have been the sickness, it could have been something else, but he was certain there were spirits in his midst, silhouettes of yester-years gliding through the grass. They were silent, faceless, yet they filled him with fear, sorrow, with agony and shame.

"Stand up."

Varésh regarded the rainswept meadow with blurry eyes. Before him stood a silhouette composed of brilliant light.

"My dearest Varésh...stand up."

The world swam back into focus and he wasn't sure whether or not he was hallucinating.

"Sonja?"

Her laugh was unmistakable. Varésh knew the moment a smile manifested on the silhouette that it was her, his beloved Sonja come to talk some sense into him—he hoped. For all he knew it was a trick of his shadow twin, a ruse to unnerve him, to further unravel his sanity and push him to the brink of utter madness.

Her touch was warm, gentle. Her smile and her eyes were as sweet as he remembered, as he had seen in dreams. Varésh reached for her but to his touch she was a ghost. How cruel a punishment that was.

"You need to stand," she said again, and helped him to his feet. *"This meadow is not the end of your journey. That, my Varésh, is a long time from now."*

He averted her gaze, shame rumbling in his gut. "I sometimes think I don't deserve to live. Not after all I've done..." He inhaled deeply, looked her in the eyes. "Not after what I did to you."

Sonja winced. Her expression soured slightly. *"I hate you for my death, Varésh. But I believe in your heart—even the worst of us, the most misguided can achieve redemption."*

Varésh swallowed the lump in his throat. Fresh tears fell from his eyes. He felt lighter for her words, yet still weighted down by his sins.

"The way forward is arduous," Sonja said. *"Far more than you can see. The game is long."*

"The game was always long," Varésh said.

"There are many pieces yet to be revealed," Sonja said. *"It is a game of shadows. I have seen the end."*

There was a tremor in her voice. Varésh frowned. "And?"

"It is not for me to tell," said Sonja. *"That is the way of things. That is fate."*

There was a long silence between them as the rain fell.

"I miss you terribly," Varésh said.

Sonja offered only a sad smile. Her form faded to mist, then she was gone.

———

IT WAS dark when Varésh finally stopped for the day. Clouds scraped the sky but they were thin and the rain had stopped. The moon shone pale and the light was soothing. It made Varésh think of home, of childhood and all the nights he had spent gazing at the stars. Simpler times. Gentler times.

He leaned against the wall of the tower ruin he had taken refuge in. Its name had long escaped him and this realization was profound. He had always feared being forgotten. The notion made him feel empty inside, made him feel like little more than a ghost. If things and people were fated for name-lessness, how important had they been to begin with?

"You," his shadow twin hissed, *"have grown so sadly intro-spective in these last years."*

Varésh ignored the jab. *My philosophical brooding is nothing new,* he thought. *Just...rediscovered. I was like this in my youth back home on Indris.* Celestials, he missed that planet so! Missed home so much it hurt—but he could not go back. *What do you care?*

"*I don't,*" his shadow twin said. "*I was merely remarking.*"

Varésh frowned and crossed his arms to his chest. *Why are you so convinced I haven't changed? You're absolutely hell-bent on believing my intentions false, on convincing me my intentions are false—why?*

"*Because I know you, Varésh Lúm-talé,*" his shadow twin said. "*More than you know yourself.*"

Again you imply autonomy, Varésh thought, *and I am reasonably sure I am real. If you are not my conscience then who or what are you?*

"*Your lie,*" his shadow twin said. "*The lie you will always carry with you. Worry not, Varésh Lúm-talé, clarity will manifest soon enough.*"

The world was silent. Varésh closed his eyes.

"'*Your lie,*'" he whispered pensively. Lies were the foundation upon which he had built his life—which one was this?

4

MANIFESTED FALSITIES

Then

VARÉSH LÚM-TALÉ WAS A GOD. At least, he fancied himself a god. Considering the power he wielded and the place from which he'd come, he was at least on par with Alerion, Mirkvahíl, and Luminíl. So, actually, yes—Varésh Lúm-talé was, in fact, a god. And with great power came great emotional instability.

He wiped the snot from his nose and took another sip of whiskey. How in the high holy fuck had it come to this? Luminíl, corrupted and running amok, sowing chaos with every step, with every flap of those great, monstrous wings. Mirkvahíl, struggling to combat her dark lover. And Alerion?

"*Fuck* Alerion," Varésh slurred. "Fuck *everything. Especially* fuck Luminíl."

If not for the Vulture then Sonja would still be alive. Condemning her to death had been the hardest thing he'd ever done, but what other option had there been? If not even Alerion or Mirkvahíl had been able to free her of Luminíl's corrupted will, then what chance did Varésh expect to have? He raised his glass to the memory of his wife then hurled it across the room. It hit the wall and shattered, glass and whiskey flying all directions.

A knock on the door. It opened before Varésh had a chance to tell whomever it was to piss off into the night. He calmed slightly at the sight of Rhona, perhaps the only other person in this city to whom he could relate. Only a week ago she had hung her beloved Djen Shy'eth, another of Luminíl's acolytes. Another soul lost to the corruptive nature of mirkúr.

"A drink?" Varésh asked as Rhona took a seat across from him.

"Please."

Varésh poured her one. She took it from him and downed it in a single gulp. It seemed that kind of thing was going around. He offered a sympathetic frown. "Know how you feel. At least I think I do. I hope I do."

Rhona leaned back in her chair. "And how do you think I feel?"

Varésh opened his mouth. "I—"

Now

"THAT'S NOT HOW IT HAPPENED," said his shadow twin, pulling Varésh from his rage.

Of course it is, Varésh snapped. *Why would it not be?*

"*Why does a jealous lover manifest falsities?*" his shadow twin asked as it took form. It extended a wispy finger to Varésh's temple and pressed, drawing a wince. "*Relax and let me kill this lie of yours. Let me show you what I saw through borrowed eyes while I was still able.*"

Then

VARÉSH DWELLED at the north-most tip of Banerowos in a home without a door. As he had mentioned to Rhona years ago, he was horribly claustrophobic.

Rhona found him in the parlor with a drink as she so often did. It made him small in the best of ways; it dismissed the general air of prestige that came with being slightly less than a god. She took a seat opposite Varésh and accepted a drink.

"You seem conflicted," Varésh said.

29

Rhona smiled ruefully. "Djen is a puzzle. She makes me question the morality of her death."

Varésh sipped his drink. "Love is strange in that respect. Profoundly powerful." He looked Rhona in the eyes. "Go on, now. Ask me what you wish—I can sense the question ravaging your mind."

"Sonja."

Varésh set his glass to the side. "She would have destroyed Jémoon."

"But she was your wife," Rhona said. "You loved her deeply."

"As you surely did Djen," Varésh said. He had a faraway look in his eyes. "I have found, in all my countless years, the right thing and the hardest thing are often times the same."

"Of course." Djen flashed across her mind. "How did you cope?"

Varésh offered a melancholy smile. He poured another drink and swirled it in his glass.

Rhona's heart sunk—actions spoke far louder than words. "I wish I could ease your pain."

Varésh reached for her hand. "And I yours." He sighed. "Reconciliation eludes me."

"In your heart of hearts, do you believe your actions right?" Rhona asked.

"Yes," Varésh said. "And no. Judgment is requisite for order, but must every criminal be hanged? Must we frown so heavily upon idealism if it makes Jémoon a better place? I cannot help wondering if perhaps there might be a flaw in the design."

"How could unity be flawed?"

Varésh stood and started from the house. Rhona followed and they came to rest at the edge of a garden overlooking Banerowos. The city was a jewel beneath the moon, its dark streets and architecture capturing celestial light. It was beautiful enough to make one momentarily forget the Vulture had been freed.

"What do you see?" Varésh asked.

"The city as she stands." Rhona tilted her head. "Should I be keen to something more?"

Varésh gave another melancholy smile. "The people. In them, what do you *really* see?"

Rhona hesitated. Was there a specific answer he was looking for?

"I see fear," said Varésh. "I see frustration. I see anger and I feel it too. I feel their emotional distress where once I did not. They crave harmony; a people united can do great things. But more than that, they desire autonomy. I hear their whispers in the night—they think the tenets too rigid. They think punishment too extreme."

Many people had been hanged for speaking out in favor of Luminíl. Many more had been hanged for less.

"If the tenets are given slack...what then?" Rhona asked. "What do you foresee?"

"Truthfully?" Varésh shrugged. "Emotion is fickle; discontent has a long memory."

Rhona tensed her jaw. Their conversation had led somewhere she had not expected; she was more conflicted than she had been upon her arrival. If Varésh of all people doubted the tenets of Jémoon, what was she to think?

"Perhaps Djen was right," Fiel said. *"Too much wine dulls the mind. Are you ever going to think for yourself? Or are you too afraid to have an opinion all your own? Deep in the confines of your mind, what do you truly believe? How do you truly feel? How have you* always *felt? What have you* always *thought?"*

Rhona swallowed. She had no immediate response. Her body tingled.

"There it is," Fiel said. *"The coldness of uncertainty creeping up your spine. Centuries of stout conviction ripped apart by the moral quandary of your almost-god. How does it feel to have lived so subservient a life?"*

"I should go," Rhona said.

Varésh nodded. He was silent as she left.

Now

"ARE you absolutely sure that's how it really went?" Varésh asked.

"*Quite,*" his shadow twin replied. "*Unlike you I am able to see the truth in madness.*"

"You were in Rhona's head," Varésh said. "How?"

His shadow twin grinned and tapped its nose. "*Truth from madness, Varésh Lúm-talé. See the truth in madness. Learn your greatest lie—only then will things become clear.*"

The shadow vanished, once more leaving Varésh alone to ponder the many lies his life had been built upon. Had any of that been real? The first dream and the last—it was possible they were real to some extent, but the fact of the matter, as it dawned on him, made Varésh cold to his bones:

Who were Rhona and Djen?

5

MOTHER WOE

MIRKVAHÍL EXUDED WARMTH. Rhona could feel it even from the first floor of her tower. Felt it more profoundly as she ascended to the pinnacle atop which the Phoenix resided. It eased her mind, pushed away the worry and anxiety of the last few days and helped her keep composure. It wasn't everyday citizens of Banerowos were granted an audience with Mirkvahíl, prominence be damned.

Mirkvahíl's quarters were radiant. She was, after all, the Phoenix—why should her dwelling not serve to further cement that fact? Like many of the other towers in the city this one too was open to the sky, possessing windows without glass and a long balcony that ran the southern length of the tower. It was there the Phoenix stood, garbed in whites and golds that fell to gossamer threads of mist. Her great wings were furled about her like a cloak and her hair fell in loose, dark curls.

"You have questions," she said as Rhona neared. "You dream but do not sleep. Fear clings to you." She turned, boring into Rhona with her pitch-black eyes. "Tell me your thoughts, Rhona. Tell me your fears. What makes you think that we were wrong to imprison Luminíl? To exact judgment on her followers as was necessary?"

Rhona frowned, joining Mirkvahíl on the balcony. "Nothing. I don't believe we were wrong. I just...want answers. Clarity. How could two people as strong-willed and logical as Djen Shy'eth and Sonja Lúm-talé fall prey to Luminíl's influence? How could they not see her unbounded power threatens the existence of this world?"

Mirkvahíl studied her, never once blinking, never once looking away. "Something deeper tugs at you, Rhona. You *do* seek answers to these questions—you have always had the best interests of this world in mind. But your heart aches. I can feel as much. 'Why Djen?' you ask yourself. 'How could I have gone through with hanging her?'"

Rhona wiped a few stray tears from her cheeks. It was the first time she had cried in who knew how long. It was a peculiar feeling. She felt vulnerable here before the Phoenix and she did not like the sensation.

Mirkvahíl took her in a gentle embrace, furling her wings around them both.

"It is normal to feel such things," the Phoenix said. "The

hurt. The confusion. The guilt. I have felt them all more and more with each passing day, each passing week and month and year. I loved Luminíl more than anything. I have felt her absence for some time, but I have also felt her phantom rage slithering through the air, unbounded like a storm. Were we right to imprison her? Were we right to favor country over person? Was there anything—*is* there anything we can do to quell her rampant mirkúr?"

Rhona said nothing as Mirkvahíl spoke. She focused only on the Phoenix's self-admitted pain, the very same she was going through. If such a creature as powerful as Mirkvahíl was having doubts then perhaps it was normal Rhona was having them too. She was, after all, wrought from the combined power of Alerion, Mirkvahíl, and Luminíl. *Everyone* was save Varésh Lúm-talé, and what must he be feeling?

"Why now?" Rhona asked. "Why express regret now after all these years?"

Mirkvahíl sighed. "Power and authority are enticing. They are seductive and profoundly so. You have felt this— that is why you are here. You need someone to whom you can relate. Idealism is a double-sided coin, Rhona. With utopia comes darkness. Every candle lit is another shadow cast. Perfection is a lie. Law requires chaos. It is a vicious circle; one I fear we have realized far too late."

"Too late?" Rhona asked, pulling back. "Too late for what?"

Mirkvahíl closed her eyes. "There is no saving Banerowos. There is no saving Jémoon."

"You can't possible know that," Rhona said. "Where there is will, there stands a chance. Luminíl's power is not so wild that it cannot be contained."

"I wish that were so," Mirkvahíl said, turning to stare out into the night.

Rhona bared her teeth in a rictus of disgust. "How can you give up so easily? If we are truly responsible for this mess then we have to do what we can to rectify it!" Mirkvahíl was silent. "How can you abandon your people so easily?"

"Luminíl and Djen might ask the same of us," Mirkvahíl said softly. "They *did* ask the same, and with what did we reply? 'I do as the Raven wills.' What a shield to hide behind. What a lie to justify our actions."

The warmth of the tower vanished. With it went the light and brilliance of Mirkvahíl until she was little more than a winged silhouette. "You came to me hoping for something else and for that I am sorry. For many things I am sorry, most of all you, Rhona. Farewell."

Disgusted, Rhona fled the tower teary-eyed and wanting desperately to shove a knife down Mirkvahíl's throat. Did she dare speak to Alerion now? Might he echo the same sentiments? Might he too concede defeat? Rhona didn't care to find out and so withdrew from Banerowos to the solace of Hang-Dead Forest.

———

WHAT DID it say about Rhona that she felt more at ease amongst the corpses in the trees than she did the majesty of Banerowos? Until tonight she had never thought to question it. Until tonight she had never thought to question many things, and the one person to whom she thought she could relate had done more harm than good.

"*You are going to do something reckless,*" Fiel said.

Is that a question or a statement? Rhona asked.

"*A bit of both,*" Fiel said. "*What sort of recklessness are you resorting to?*"

The expensive kind, said Rhona. *Some think my reverence of the trees overzealous—I will prove them wrong. Every action has a purpose, realized or not; every purpose has a price. Tonight my scarlet coinage grants an audience with the dead.*

Fiel gasped. "*Such an act is forbidden.*"

A lot of things are forbidden, Rhona said. *That doesn't necessarily make them wrong.*

"How desperate you must be to have strayed from your path, little rule-follower," Fiel hissed. "Have you begun rewriting your articles of faith or are you simply grasping at straws?"

Rhona came to the Lost Tree from which Djen and so many others hung. It groaned in a breeze; bodies danced their pendulum dance. For a moment she imagined holding Djen, the pair swaying on the shore of the lake.

You seek the hang-dead dream, said the Lost Tree.

Rhona knelt and bowed her head. "Blood paid is a debt owed."

Indeed, said the Lost Tree, *and you have given much. I will grant you access to the dream, but know that what is written cannot be erased.*

"I understand." Rhona closed her eyes.

Be still, now, said the tree. *Be as the souls you seek. And remember my words—*

This is more than a dream.

———————

THE LOST TREE was not the first to relay to Rhona the notion dreams were sometimes more than what they seemed. Such a thought was a favorite of the being Equilibrium whom Rhona had conversed with many times before. Still, this time around she couldn't help but feel...different. As if the Silent Place—to which the Lost Tree had surely delivered her cognizance—had manifested from within and engulfed her. As if it were calling out, trying to become one.

She turned about the darkness she had woken to, each step reverberating softly, each movement leaving an ethereal echo in its wake. The way forward was not certain; Rhona wasn't remotely sure what she was looking for in this instant. Djen, Sonja, any of the Hang-Dead souls were whom she sought but the question now was how to find them.

"*Mirkvahil always had a saying,*" said Fiel. "*Do you recall? 'In the darkest night the faintest light is blinding.' Draw upon yourself to illuminate the path. This is, after all, a conjuration of your mind. At least, as the Silent Place interprets what you seek.*"

Rhona held an upturned palm out to the nothingness. Gradually small beads of light coalesced at her finger tips, braiding inward until they formed a sphere of pale blue illumination. It ascended and the darkness bled away in rivulets just as it had the last time she had come. Instead of a silver meadow she found herself before the ruin of a temple, the sky above a pallid swirl of clouds.

"What is this place?" Rhona asked, mostly to herself, but partly to the ruin.

Fiel hissed.

Do you know where we are? Rhona asked. She took a step toward the threshold; Fiel snarled. *Spit it out.*

"*This is* her *realm,*" said Fiel. "*They call her Mother Woe.*"

Rhona had never heard of Mother Woe. *Where did you learn that?*

"*Through exploration,*" said Fiel. "*You and I are one and the same. In the rarest of instances I do have autonomy.*"

Imagine my shock. Rhona rolled her eyes. *Explain to me this Mother Woe. Why are you so afraid of her? What is she?*

"*Dangerous,*" said Fiel. "*As was Luminil to Alerion, as Chaos is to Balance, Mother Woe is to Equilibrium.*" The temple door creaked ajar. "*It seems she has been expecting you. Be vigilant. Be receptive to her words. As the Lost Tree said—this is more than just a dream."*

Rhona crossed into the temple, overcome by the scent of old stone and dirt. Of rain.

Of mirkúr.

She thought to conjure a blade but the notion fled as quickly as it'd come. She knew it was purely out of fear, a means of a defense, but she doubted Mother Woe would see it that way. Best to come unarmed to such an amphitheater of uncertainty, especially if its mistress was as powerful as Fiel had said.

The anteroom was long and wide, its ceiling arched. It had once been beautiful. Beyond the crumbling stone and lichens, past the dust and mold, were faded, fragmented inlays illustrating winged beings numbering in the hundreds. What had this place been built in reverence to?

The anteroom yawned into a circular courtyard bordered by tall white-leaved trees. Motes of light and shadow wafted through the air like snowflakes. Had the temple itself not been so glum Rhona might have found the scene beautiful.

"And here I thought you found solace in death," Fiel jabbed.

Rhona ignored the voice.

A faint melody tickled her ears. She trained her hearing to the words—it was coming just beyond the trees. She marched through the courtyard and into the woods, the song growing louder, more intelligible all the while. It was infectiously sad. The nearer she grew the darker she felt. By the time she withdrew from the woods and found herself staring at a stone altar, her cheeks were stained with tears and her eyes were so pained from crying she was ready to gouge them out.

"Now, child. Keep your hands to your side." The voice was gentle yet imposing, physical yet at the same time trapped between the fabric of the world. *"You have need of sight for as long as you are here. How else will you trail your sins? How else will you behold the majesty of your monstrousness?"*

Rhona swallowed her pain. She stumbled, nearly tumbling forward, but managed to regain her balance as a lithe silhouette manifested in a swirl of smoke. She bore a black cloak and hood; tattered bird wings trailed behind her and her eyes were two full moons encircled by dark veins and peeling flesh.

Rhona fell to her knees. *"D-Djen?"*

The woman offered a melancholy smile. *"I have not used that name in...centuries. I am called mother woe and I am here to point you on your way."*

Rhona's mind was a jumble of confusion. Mother Woe was *Djen?* What did she mean she hadn't used that name in centuries? Rhona pushed herself to stand. She was dizzy as she rose to meet Mother Woe's eyes. This place felt a blur.

"*You have questions to which you seek answers,*" Mother Woe said. "*I could posit my own but what good would that do you?*" She held a hand out to Rhona. "*The way ahead is treacherous for those unprepared.*"

Rhona hesitated. "How do I know you aren't lying?"

"*You don't,*" Mother Woe said plainly. "*But what choice do you have but to trust me, the warden of this place? I can give you what Mirkvahíl could not.*"

There was venom in that last sentence, decades of subtext. But Rhona *needed* answers and she was sure lashing out physically at Mother Woe would lead nowhere good.

Rhona took her hand. It was frigid. There was not a modicum of warmth to be felt. Rhona's heart dropped at that but she couldn't bring herself to be angry at Mother Woe, at Djen. She felt only sadness and an inkling of regret.

"Where do we go from here?" Rhona asked.

"*The Bone Garden,*" Mother Woe said.

They started for the trees, crossed the threshold into a dark wood illuminated by tiny motes of light. Normally such a place would have made Rhona feel at ease. The manifestation of corpses, wayward souls, and twisted trees would have made her feel as though she had done the right thing, what the Raven had willed. But here, beside Mother Woe, all it did was fill her with dread. What was this place? Who were these sorry, white-eyed corpses hanging from trees? Who and what were all these wailing, gossamer spirits?

"You will learn," Mother Woe said as if she had read Rhona's thoughts. *"In time you will learn. For now, simply walk and ruminate on everything you have been, are, and want to be."*

6

FATHER SKY

Then

R HONA HAD ALWAYS HAD a soft spot for Alerion. To all of Jémoon he was the Raven, a third of the great creators of Harthe. Secretly, to Rhona, he was Father Sky, a parental figure for a woman who had simply come to be, like so many others of her kind. Yet she found herself questioning his judgment. So many Jémoonites had voiced their opposition to his jailing of Luminíl; for that they now hung from the branches of the Raven's Wood.

You aided Alerion, Rhona thought to herself as she stared at the lake. *Don't forget that. You went along with his decision. You were a willing participant.* She looked at her hands, at her forearms, at the reflection of her face, all caked in dried blood. *Was it worth it? All that death... I do as the Raven wills but...*

Rhona sighed. She had never felt so conflicted before. She loved Alerion, admired his character, but she had also been friends with Luminíl, with many of the Jémoonites who risen up against Alerion and Mirkvahíl and lost their lives.

Rhona turned at a soft breeze against her back. Alerion stood there, midnight-feathered wings furled around him like a cloak. His gray eyes shone even without the aid of the moonlight. He offered a small smile, one that seemed to suggest his sympathy.

Rhona stood to face him, arms wrapped around herself. She chewed her lower lip, eyes narrowed pensively. "I want to believe our course of action was the right one. I *need* to believe, to know that Luminíl's continued freedom would have left the world prey to unbounded mirkúr. That jailing her was the kindest thing we could have done."

"Child." Alerion neared her. He cupped her cheek; his hand was warm and it eased her mind. "So often I have found the right thing to be the hardest. It breaks my heart. I can scarcely imagine everything that might be running through Luminíl's mind, through the citizens of Banerowos...but I take solace knowing we have quelled the threat of complete annihilation."

Rhona couldn't ignore that fact. The cage in which Luminíl now resided kept her rampant energies at bay while still allowing the Jémoonites to draw from her mirkúr as they drew illum from Mirkvahíl.

That somehow makes this feel worse. Rhona felt sick at the thought of Luminíl being little more than a source from which parasites drew strength.

"Was there truly no other way?" she asked Alerion.

He shook his head and his face caught briefly in the moonlight. His cheeks were tear-stained and his eyes red. "Mirkvahíl and I could find no other solution. I pray one presents itself in time; I do not wish to see Luminíl imprisoned eternally."

Yet your tone suggests the possibility of such a thing is great, Rhona thought.

"You are covered in blood," Alerion noted. "Why have you not yet cleaned yourself?"

Rhona bowed her head. "Shame. Guilt, I suppose."

"Both are reasonable responses," Alerion said, "but I see no shame in defending the livelihood of your people, of your home. The dead knew what they were doing; they rose up in favor of Luminíl despite Mirkvahíl and myself wishing things to be as peaceful as possible."

"Maybe violence was the most peaceful option," Rhona said. "I hardly think a being so powerful as Luminíl would enjoy being locked away, even willingly."

Alerion's expression darkened. "She was not—Luminíl has always been a bit difficult. It saddens me to say I foresaw her response. She always favored power slightly more than she did the lives of her people." Alerion tensed his jaw. "...She tried to kill Mirkvahíl some time ago."

Rhona's eyes widened.

"Not purposely, not entirely," Alerion said. "It was years back, when her temperance first began to wane."

"What would have caused her to do such a thing?" Rhona asked. "She and Mirkvahíl..."

"Were lovers, yes," Alerion said. "Mirkvahíl and I have been fruitless in our attempts to find an answer to her illness. What little we know is that it makes her lose control. It...eats away at her compassion, at her control."

"Entropy destroying Entropy," said Rhona. "It would be ironic if it wasn't so horrible. How many others know?"

"The whole of Jémoon," Alerion said. "It would be foolish for Mirkvahíl and I to conceal something of such import. And yet..." He heaved a sigh. "I know it will not deter her acolytes from trying to free her. I laud them for their dedication to Luminíl—it is plain to see she meant a great deal to a great many people. But I curse their blind allegiance, too. Releasing the Vulture from her cage will do more harm than good."

They were both silent for a time, Rhona letting Alerion's words sink into her head. Jémoon and Banerowos were still in their infancy. Country and city had come so far in just decades yet peace and growth had devolved into civil war and the notion of utter and complete destruction. Rhona had never once dreamed things would crumble so dramatically, if at all. Never once had she dreamt of utopia and dystopia being one and the same.

"What would you have me do?" she asked finally.

"See the bigger picture," Alerion said softly. "Country over person, Rhona. As difficult a tenet as it seems, it is the one we must live by if Jémoon is to survive. Alf elo nor, nor elo alf. Do you understand?"

Alf elo nor—one for all. Nor elo alf—all for one.

Rhona nodded.

Then

"TWELVE IN A SINGLE EVENING," said Varésh. "A new record."

"A new post-war record," Rhona said as they watched the blood-stained corpses dance their pendulum dance. She dragged her blade across the palm of her hand and pressed it to the earth, whispering, *"Alf elo nor."* It was her twelfth cut of the night.

"You do that more than most," Varésh said. "Actually, you might very well be the *only* one who does it. Giving blood to Hang-Dead Forest, I mean."

Rhona shrugged. "It might do you well to mimic me,

Varésh. Reverence goes a long way in a place like this. Blood paid is a debt owed."

Varésh snorted. "What could the trees possibly have to give?"

"Whatever they deem worthy of my blood," Rhona said, bandaging her hand. "Who knows? My sanguine reverence may yet save Jémoon, and then would you be questioning my many scars?" They numbered in the hundreds. A cut for every corpse. The more that hung, the more Rhona bled; the more she bled, the closer she grew to complete exaltation with Hang-Dead Forest. Her gut told her this was right, that someday everything she had given would be repaid tenfold. She hoped it meant peace, harmony at last.

"What does Mirkvahíl think of you shedding blood so freely? Alerion?" Varésh asked. He was a bit green in the face.

"They agree with it," Rhona said. "In fact, it was Alerion who first suggested doing so."

"A bit...macabre," Varésh said. "The Raven, wise as he may be, has become a bit dark these last several years. A bit more...oh, shit—what's the phrase I'm looking for?" He snapped his fingers repeatedly. "Superstitious. I think."

Rhona cocked an eyebrow. "Superstitious?"

"Alerion never used to be this obsessed with death," Varésh said.

"I would hardly call putting Jémoon's best interests at heart 'superstitious,' Varésh," Rhona said. "We do as the Raven wills. If Luminíl's acolytes are going to continue threatening harmony with their individualistic nonsense then what better recourse is there than to snuff them out? Utopia is only attainable if everyone is working toward the same goal."

Varésh sighed. "I suppose you're right." He shuddered. "Can we go?"

"Fine," Rhona said, and they started back toward Banerowos.

Then

"IT HAD TO BE DONE, VARÉSH." Rhona squeezed his shoulder. "I'm to lead Djen to her end a fortnight from now. I... know how you feel. I hope."

Varésh said nothing as he watched his wife, Sonja, swing from the Lost Tree.

"She and Djen freed Luminíl from her prison," Rhona continued, not knowing what else to do but preach the sins of their beloveds. "They may have very well doomed Jémoon— Harthe, even—to its end."

"I know." Varésh was hoarse. He had clearly spent the previous night screaming. "We do..." He sniffled, then tense his jaw. "We do as the Raven wills. If only Sonja and Djen had seen sense to do the same." He bowed his head, muttering indiscernibly.

"Power corrupts," Rhona said. "If it was not plain to see before then it surely is now." The words were meant more for her than they were Varésh. Sonja had always been outspoken where Luminíl's imprisonment was concerned, but Rhona had never thought she would do something so rash as releasing the Vulture. She had never once dreamed Djen would be swayed to such recklessness, either.

Fuck.

"I suppose...I suppose I never really knew Sonja as well as I thought. My own *wife*, conspiring to sentence Jémoon to its end." A guttural scream escaped his lips and Varésh sent a thread of illum javelining upward through the trees and into the night.

Rhona took his hand and squeezed. "Come on. A drink will do you some good."

It would do *her* some good as well. She had a fortnight to rid herself of her emotional attachment to Djen. It was best to start now.

Now

"*I WONDER IF YOU REALLY KNOW*..." Mother Woe said, snapping Rhona from her pensive trance.

"Know what?" Rhona asked.

Mother Woe smiled and said nothing else.

Rhona had no clue as to how long they had been walking through this awful, twisted forest. Fiel had been utterly silent, quelled by the presence of Mother Woe, of what had once been Djen...centuries ago, whatever that meant.

"Time is complex," Mother Woe said. *"Memory is complex. Amalgamate them and you might very well lose your mind trying to put the pieces in the right order. no one ever said parables were harmless."*

"Is that what this is? Some sort of lesson?" Rhona asked.

"In a manner of speaking," Mother Woe said. *"If you really think about it your entire existence has been a parable, Rhona. one could say the same of alerion as well, the fool. What a lie he is."*

Rhona refrained from asking what Mother Woe meant. She knew the response she'd get.

At length, the forest bled into a pitch black night. Before them a stone bridge stretched the length of a massive chasm. At its other side stood an old gate and a wall of mirkúr, bone, and stone.

"What is it?"

"The birth place of clarity," Mother Woe said. *"The bone garden."* She gestured toward the bridge. Her hood fell back and her dark hair whipped about her face in a gust of cold air. Amidst her ruin, in the depths of her eyes, Rhona could see a hint of the woman she had loved, the woman she had hung. Her heart twinged.

"Am I to go alone?"

Mother Woe nodded. *"Farewell."* She took a step back and dropped into the chasm below.

Rhona wrapped her arms around herself and swallowed.

"What a horrible place this is," Fiel said, startling Rhona.

I...I don't want to cross that bridge, Rhona thought.

"You must," Fiel said. Its dread was evident. *"You seek answers."*

Rhona heaved a sigh. *Oh, Djen... What the hell have I gotten myself into?*

She started across the bridge.

7

FOREST DARK

THERE WAS a profound correlation between morality, truth, and the lies one told oneself. Varésh had spent the last few days ruminating in silence—thank the Celestials for *that*—on Rhona and Djen, on their significance in what he had seen in his dream. It was certainly within the realm of possibility they and the dream were mere conjurations of his shadow twin, an attempt to further unhinge Varésh. To further blur the line between reality and falsity.

But something in him told Varésh there was more to the women, that they were connected yet to the Phoenix Mirkvahíl. His shadow twin's claim of having infiltrated Rhona's dreams suggested as much, suggested, at the very least, Varésh and Rhona had fought for a common goal. The only problem was Varésh, long as his memory was, could not remember once having that conversation, let alone speaking with Rhona.

"Trees," said Varésh as he crossed the threshold into a dense wood. "Thank the Celestials for trees." He had seen nothing but grass and ruins the last few days; this was a welcome change of pace. Or would have been if not for the myriad bones protruding from and hanging from the trees. "Fuck."

Hang-Dead Forest had never been Varésh's favorite locale but that was something he was going to have to stomach if he wanted to reach Mirkvahíl. Her song had grown increasingly louder the last day or so, to the point it had become a low and constant ringing in his ears. Varésh sighed; reluctantly he took the path at a measured pace, conjuring a tiny mote of illum to guide his way. It had been a long time since last he had come to Hang-Dead Forest, longer yet since this place had been free of its ever-present darkness.

"Why the fuck..." Varésh didn't need to finish the question to know the answer. The lust for power and the idea of utopia pushed people to barbarism, to nationalistic atrocities. "How could we have ever thought it was right?"

He stopped before a trio of skeletons hanging from a lower branch. One of the skeletons was far smaller than the other two, not yet fully developed. Varésh swallowed the bile rising in his throat and cursed himself a thousand times over.

I have to fix this, he thought.

"You have to do a lot of things," his shadow twin whis-

pered. *"There is much to be done to achieve even a modicum of hope to right your wrongs, Varésh Lúm-talé."*

Varésh's upper lip curled. *You are the most back and forth monstrosity I have ever had the misfortune of conversing with. Which is it—do you want me to succeed or do you want me to fail? It seems to me you would find more joy in the latter.*

"On the contrary. *Nothing would please me more than to see Harthe spared your idiocy,"* his shadow twin said. *"You will learn the truth of things in time, that much is known, but as your Sonja said: the way ahead is arduous."*

And I suppose part of the experience of failure is dealing with my demons, guilt, and manifested falsities, thought Varésh. *All of which you seem to exacerbate.*

"*I must do* something *to pass the time in here,"* his shadow twin hissed. *"I have seen your every thought and dream a thousand times over. There is little else I can do but goad you on your way, Varésh Lúm-talé. For what it is worth, this is as much a learning experience for me as it is for you."*

Varésh said nothing as he continued through Hang-Dead Forest.

"Do you remember when you hung me here?"

The voice pulled Varésh from a long and meandering recollection about Sonja. He looked about, spied her luminescent silhouette in a clearing several yards ahead. He swallowed, choking back tears as the memory took like a flame to paper.

"How could I forget?"

He had dreamt it every night in the years since Sonja's violent end. Since he had murdered her for having differing beliefs. It was penance for his actions, but not penance enough. Nothing would ever be punishment enough for what he had done to his wife.

"*You could have stopped this all, Vare,*" Sonja lamented. She danced away from him, winding through the trees like a leaf on a breeze. Varésh gave chase. "*You could have been great. We could have been such keepers of this planet...*"

Varésh came to a sliding halt as Sonja vanished.

"*But you could never deny your father,*" the trees taunted in her voice.

"*Always had to prove yourself.*"

"*Always had to fuck things up—didn't you?*"

"Didn't you?"

Dɪᴅɴ'ᴛ ʏᴏᴜ?

DIDN'T YOU?

Sonja manifested in a burst of shadow, a grating shriek erupting from elongated jowls, eyes like wan full moons. She swiped at him with taloned fingers and it was all Varésh could do to avoid her fury. He stumbled backward, nearly tripped over his own feet as he shaped his illum mote into a thin, radiant blade. Sonja hissed at its warmth; its light revealed the utter ruin of her countenance, peeling flesh and all.

"Celestials..." Varésh whimpered, feebly but successfully deflecting another enraged swipe, *"what have I done?"*

"*Look at me,*" Sonja snarled. "*Look at me, Varésh. look upon the manifestation of your lies. You are a fool if you think finding Mirkvahíl can remedy this. You are a fool if you believe the lie you have sold yourself. Some things are simply set in stone.*"

"I can redeem myself," Varésh said, brushing away his tears. "I *can.* I *must,* Sonja."

She struck again; this time the blow landed with force. Talons raked across Varésh's face and he fell to the ground in a daze. His blood was warm against his flesh, soothing as Hang-Dead Forest spun in and out of focus, as the specter of his beloved Sonja knelt and tugged upon his spirit. Her mirkúr wormed its way to the center of his chest, of his mind and he saw light.

———

VARÉSH BLINKED AND the world was still. He stood before a lake. Its surface collected starlight as a net would fish. It was beautiful and it made him feel at peace.

"This isn't right," he murmured, the image of Sonja's ruined corpse fresh in his mind. He had been in Hang-Dead

Forest. Then he had seen a light far brighter than anything before him now. Sunlight? Moonlight?

"That is a very astute observation."

Varésh watched the lake manifest his shadow twin. There was something different about it this time, something more... whole and realized. The storm-gray eyes, the sharpness of its jawline, and...

"Shit."

The midnight, feathered wings he had seen so many times before. As they burst forth from his shadow twin's back so too did they sprout from Varésh, pushing through his flesh and procuring a shriek, completing his lie.

"You wear me sadly," said Alerion. "Like a cutthroat does a crown achieved by spilling blood." He smirked at Varésh's discomfort. "I told you clarity would come to you soon enough. And worry not—all is yet to be revealed."

Varésh had a long memory but none of this registered. How had he come to wear Alerion's guise? What had happened to Alerion?

"Is this another trick?" he asked. "What is this place? Why am I here?"

"No, not a trick," Alerion said. "I am not so cruel as that. I am not so cruel as you, Varésh Lúm-talé. As you are wont to ravage lives, I am sworn to save them—that is what I have done for you. Saved you from the product of your arrogance."

"Sonja."

"She is just one of many bent by death, by the touch of

wild mirkúr," Alerion said. "A rusalk. A once preventable monstrosity now numbering in the hundreds of thousands." Alerion shook his head and heaved a sigh. "Power is fool's gold, Varésh. Do you see now what it does? The ruin of this world and its people is the very same that fate will deliver unto Indris, unto your father and your people."

Varésh bowed his head. "I have seen—I have known this for a time. It is why I *must* find Mirkvahíl. To make things right, to quell the destruction Luminíl has wrought. To save her. To...to..." He steeled himself and looked Alerion in the eyes. "To be better, *different from* my father. To be a *true* Architect. To rear and nurture worlds, not remake them in my image. Please."

Alerion frowned. "There is passion in your words, Varésh Lúm-talé. Sincerity wrought from guilt. But even if you are able to find Mirkvahíl I fear she will be of little use to your cause. I have seen her soul and it is shattered. Her mind is lost."

"Still, I have to try," Varésh said.

"I know. The way ahead is dangerous," Alerion said. "There are things you will learn that have the power to destroy you."

"Rightfully so," Varésh murmured.

"Indeed." Alerion held his hand out to Varésh. His expression softened and for a moment Varésh swore he saw a hint of sympathy in that gray stare. "When you are ready I will deliver you from sleep. Stay vigilant."

Varésh took Alerion's hand and the lake-world melted away in rivulets.

He awoke in Hang-Dead Forest with a gasp.

———

Varésh's face burned something fierce. He ran his fingers gingerly along the lacerations. They had closed of their own volition, scarred; Sonja's talons had also missed his eyes and he drank the darkness in. It was beautiful.

"*Stand,*" Alerion commanded, once more a voice in Varésh's head.

Varésh stood, ears trained to a distant song, that of the Phoenix Mirkvahíl. He was growing closer; his quarry, his destiny was perhaps only hours away on the other side of Hang-Dead Forest.

Where is Sonja? he asked of Alerion.

"*About,*" Alerion said. "*They* all *are.*"

A shiver crept up Varésh's spine. He had failed to quell Sonja's wrath—how did he expect to best *all* the rusalks? How many did *all* even mean? He supposed it didn't matter. He would either reach his destination or he would die trying. It was all part of the experience of failure. It was all part of redemption, and Celestials, did Varésh want to be redeemed.

He steeled his nerves and walked.

8

IMPOSTER SYNDROME

Then

VARÉSH LÚM-TALÉ HAD NEVER SEEN A PLANET SO beautiful as Harthe, Harmony in the Celestial tongue. This celestial sphere in all its splendor—it was *his* to mold, his to remake in a manner of speaking. Some planets were little more than spherical scenery, devoid of any sentient life. Others were blooming. And then there were some, like Harthe, wrought from their own unique pillars of creation yet, for whatever reason, needing that extra nudge.

Varésh had always wanted to nudge and now he had the perfect opportunity—*if* the locals saw fit to accept his aid. He walked the grassland, hands behind his back, nose keen to the sweet perfume of myriad flowers riding on the wind. To his left sat a great lake, placid, like a mirror or a doorway to an inverse world.

"So much I could do here," he mused. "What a world I could make of Harmony. It could be the greatest restoration, the greatest maturation in Celestial history. Orchestrated by me, a novice Architect."

So many times Varésh had fantasized about getting his chance to prove himself to his people and their emperor, his father. There were many who believed Varésh had been given this responsibility simply because of his birthright, but if they *really* knew Ouran, really knew what made him tick, they would realize Varésh had been anything but his favored son. In fact, at times, Varésh had felt he *wasn't* Ouran's son. Ouran was a man of vision. Varésh had...pieces of visions, and that was about it. Ambition but without the wherewithal to capitalize on his intent.

Until now. His power surged at the notion. The energy, radich, swam through him like an eager serpent toward its prey. *So much possibility,* Varésh thought. What would his radich take the form of here? What energies did these great pillars of creation wield? Varésh salivated at the thought, at the anticipation. He *needed* to know. He burned to.

And yet... He couldn't ignore the tiny voice in the back of his mind, chiding the Celestials and the emulative nature of radich—*possibility* in the Celestial vernacular. There were, unfortunately, many a Celestial Architects through the

history of Indris who had used their power for lesser, more...
unconscionable things.

But I will not be one of them, Varésh thought, dropping to
his knees and closing his eyes.

"I will not."

Now

RETROSPECTION WAS both enlightening and frightening.
Varésh remembered well the first time he had set foot on
Harthe, the first time he had breathed its sweet air. The first
time a vision for what this planet could be had manifested
wholly in his mind. All of that seemed so very long ago. A dot
of light in what had otherwise been a stumble through darkness and uncertainty.

"*Do you know what I find most interesting?*" Alerion
asked. "*About you as you were then and you as you are now? A
sense of hope, dedication wrought not from a hungering for
control, but from the desire to make things better.*"

I suppose it's good someone *sees that,* Varésh thought. *All
I see is a fool.*

"*We are all of us fools at some point in our lives,*" Alerion
said. "*Myself included.*"

Varésh wasn't sure what Alerion meant by that. He

brushed it from his mind and continued through Hang-Dead Forest, vigilant to every sound, spooked by every cracking twig or gust of wind. He almost wished Sonja and the other rusalks would show themselves. Then, at the very least, he would know what pitiful things were watching him.

Do you recall ever knowing anyone named Rhona or Djen? Varésh asked. *You showed me a conversation with myself from Rhona's perspective but...*

"You still can't recall having ever met either of them," Alerion said. *"You can thank Luminíl's unbounded mirkúr for those gaps in your memory. It magnifies the guilt and that in turn magnifies repression."*

So how is it I have come to remember what I have on this journey? Varésh asked.

"I am balance," Alerion said. *"I both destroy and preserve. Think of it as...removing mental blocks."*

I suppose that makes sense, Varésh thought. He was more damaged than he had first thought. Rightfully so. After everything he had done why would he *want* to remember any of that? It was like Alerion said—truths were often times lies one told oneself. The Sonja he had first met in the meadow, her sweetness and confidence in him, had been a lie. Fuck,Varésh's very *guise* was a lie. How many more truths had he fabricated? What monstrosities yet awaited him?

At length he came to a small clearing. In its center was an effigy. He knew in his gut he should recognize it, knew it should make him feel *something*—but he could not, and it did not. He stood there, staring at the eldritch thing, little more than a hood and robe from which protruded six great wings.

"What have I forgotten?" he asked the effigy. "What shame have I repressed?"

The statue seemed to *shift* at his words. The forest dilated, leaving Varésh and the effigy in a void neither dark nor light but rather both at once. He felt dizzy, nauseous. What was this? Where was he? *What* was he?

Desolator. Woe Bringer, said the statue. *As we have epithets so too do you, Varésh Lúm-talé. you Are the very definition of your name—did your father never tell you what your name translates to? Falsity. You have always been a lie. From the time of your birth, until the day you die, and for eternity, you will always be a lie.*

Fragments of stone exploded outward from the effigy, revealing the towering monstrosity within. Dark as night, six feathered wings, and an orb of stark white light where a face should sit. It reached for Varésh and plucked him from where he stood with its thumb and index finger.

Like a carrion bird to a corpse, I will devour you, it said. I will eat your pretense. And you will know. Everything.

It held him over its luminescent face; the light dilated to reveal a cavernous void.

Varésh shrieked as he fell.

———

THIS WILL BE THE SECOND worst thing you learn of yourself.

You walk the streets of Banerowos with intent born of desire. You tell yourself you are doing this thing because you wish only to nurture Harthe to greatness, whatever that may be; that is not yet known to you. You tell yourself you do this thing because only you and you alone know how to save this infinitesimal world. You are an Architect. You were born for this—it is in your very blood.

The night is cold and your blood runs hot with anticipation. You tell yourself you were sent here for a reason. Alerion, Mirkvahíl, and Luminíl...they require guidance, they require molding. They must see things as you do lest they destroy this orb they call their home, their creation. Things have gone well enough but there is always room for error. if only they could see...

"The right thing is often times the hardest," you whisper to yourself. You urge yourself to believe it, though deep in the bowels of your existence, in that nook in which some semblance of your conscience still remains, you know that this is wrong. Why else would it be so difficult?

You come to the lake you so often times find yourself staring into. It is beautiful as always. It makes you think of home, of Indris in a way. So many stars collecting in that placid surface, so many possibilities.

"Varésh. well met," Alerion greets. He stands before the lake, hands clasped behind his back. His eyelids are heavy and he wears a soft smile; he has had a good day. "How are you this evening? What brings you here?"

"Well," you reply, mimicking his posture. "Just...admiring the lake as I am wont to do."

"She is a sight," Alerion says. His storm-gray eyes shine bright without the aid of light and his shoulder-length raven hair is pulled back behind his ears. His wings hang limply from his back, touching the grass beneath his feet. How beautiful they are. How beautiful a thing Alerion is.

"Harthe has come a way these years," you say. It is true. There has been great progress where the evolution of harmony is concerned. Banerowos is a jewel. Jémoon is... something you cannot put words to. But you love it dearly. "Still, I find myself fearful, wary. I dread the tipping of the scale."

"It is a necessary thing," Alerion says. "Without destruction there can be no evolution."

"Easy for you to say." You sigh. You feel a tickle in your throat. "You are balance made manifest. That all makes sense to you. I just..." You have seen so much destruction. You have seen worlds annihilated, you have seen people slaughtered, and for what? A witness to chaos without the power to prevent it. "I cannot let that be. It is possible to evolve without destroying what we have built. Preservation is always an option."

Your radich burns inside of you. Burns so hot it makes you cold. It hurts like nothing you have ever known, But it is a price you must pay. You concentrate, pushing the energy into the blade beneath your cloak. Urging your radich, willing it to shift, to manifest itself as mirkúr. Tears well in your eyes and you swallow the lump in your throat. You don't know if you are ready for this—but you must be. You must have strength.

You have never killed a god before.

Quick as lightning you draw the blade and thrust it into Alerion's chest, piercing bone and punching through his heart. He wears surprise as you bring him to the grass, as you cradle him in your lap.

"This is for the best," you whisper, you urge yourself to believe amidst the distant, muffled shriek from the abyss of your existence. "Forgive me."

Forgive you—for the blade you've buried in his chest and for the atrocity you have been conjuring this entire time. Alerion turns to ash without a word. You stand to admire your reflection in the lake and smile.

You will make a better god, a better creator than Alerion ever could.

You will make a better Alerion than he ever could.

———

VARÉSH FLAILED IN THE DARKNESS. Shrieked and tore at his eyes, at everything he was.

The worst is yet to come, the statue hissed. *I will break you a thousand times over. And when I am done, Varésh Lúm-*

talé...I will do it all again. Over and over. For as long as you
may live.

He was drowning, now. Liquid filled his lungs.

The darkness grew.

Then Varésh saw a man.

————

"NERÓSH."

You reach for the man. He puts a steadying hand on your
arm. You are dying. He and the rest of your acolytes have
done their best these last months but the end is inevitable.
Your end is inevitable. The empire is on the brink of collapse;
Indris wilts beneath a shroud of civil war and parasites
unleashed from Celestials know where.

"Nerósh," you murmur. He has been your loyalist follower
for as long as you can recall, the person whom you trust above
all others; he is your friend. You have very few of those left, if
you ever had any at all.

"Ouran'il will soon be overrun," Nerósh says. You notice
the blood dripping down his face, the signs of battle on his
garb. "But...we have found a way." The way he says those
words, the glint in his orange eyes... "A way to ensure you
carry on. It is untested but—"

"Do it," you say. If there is even a chance, you must take it.
The empire must survive; the seeds of resurrection must be
sown. "Whatever it is, whatever the cost, Nerósh...please."

Such a foreign word, that. You have never pled for anything in your life."

Nerósh bows his head, touches his left shoulder in salute. "As you command, Majesty." He looks up, looks you dead in the eyes, bores into you with a stare that says more than words ever could. "It has been an honor, Ouran."

There is a burst of light, scalding, shrieking, horrible.

Chaos.

Muffled annihilation.

You are hurtling through...something. Through madness.

The velocity flays you.

You are screaming muscle.

You are howling bone.

You are...weightless. A ghost among the stars. A spectator above the pandemonium and ruin of Indris, of Ouran'il, the city you built so long ago. You cry phantom tears; they drip down phantom cheeks.

Your memories shift and crack. All fades to black.

A blackness unlike anything you have ever known.

Then, a light.

A lake. Your reflection gazes up at you. You are Nerósh, but you are not. You are Ouran, but you do not remember. You are something else, someone else, with memories from a childhood of yore.

You are Varésh Lúm-talé, son of Ouran.

You are the greatest lie of all.

· · ·

VARÉSH HAD NEVER RETCHED SO MUCH in his life. This was surely a trick of the mind, this eldritch entity trying to break him with falsities. It had to be. He *needed it* to be. He was not his father, he was not and never *had been* Ouran, Celestial Emperor of Indris—right?

"R-R...*ight?*" he wheezed.

I told you I would break you, Varésh Lúm-talé. I told you the worst was yet to come and now you know, the entity said. *Now you know the extent of your lie. You were never meant to nurture Harthe to greatness—your past made it so. It is in your blood, your bones, your soul to conquer in your given name. You are vanity made manifest, arrogance in the flesh, and I am here to put you in your place. You will lose your mind.*

From the darkness came that awful, faceless orb of light. Blinding. Searing. Spellbinding.

See your lies, Varésh Lúm-talé, it hissed. *See the ruin you have caused. See them die—each and every one of them. See your Sonja as she flails from her noose—*

The entity shrieked. Its light dimmed and an ethereal figure took shape, threads of illum and mirkúr streaming outward from its feathered wings to quell the hostility.

Alerion...

"This is not the way," Alerion said.

The entity snarled, raging against its tethers. *You know well what imprisoning me does. Why stoke entropy to save this...this thing, this lie of a man?*

"Balance," Alerion said. The energies surged and the brilliance of his wings began to fade.

The darkness exploded with a howl. When the chaos cleared Varésh was kneeling before the effigy in the clearing in the woods.

"That...what—was that—?"

"Luminíl," Alerion confirmed. "A manifestation of her at least, tied to this sorry place. Stand, Varésh Lúm-talé. You must find Mirkvahíl. If we hope to have even the slightest chance of tempering Luminíl, of righting your atrocities, we must find the Phoenix before it is too late."

Varésh pushed himself to stand. His knees knocked together and his stomach threatened to empty itself further. He didn't know what to think anymore, of himself, of anything, of anything he had done. Was this quest, this undertaking to find the Phoenix even worth it? Was he worthy of being in the presence of Mirkvahíl or would the truth of his existence gradually, unconsciously force him to commit such a string of atrocities again?

Just...try, he urged himself. *Do something instead of standing here, wallowing in your failure.*

So he walked.

Mirkvahíl's song grew louder.

9

DEAR INSANITY

Aᴛ ᴏɴᴇ ᴘᴏɪɴᴛ in her life Rhona would have found the Bone Garden a place of beauty. To sit amongst and converse with the ruined dead was a privilege, the peace provided by the garden second to none.

Now, here in *this* place? Every fiber of her being screamed to turn around, to flee through those gates of bone and mirkúr and hurry across the bridge, to never come back. Guilt was such a powerful thing and it was all Rhona could do to persevere, to continue into the garden depths as muffled cries and moans rang out around her like a song she once had known and loved.

"Find strength," Fiel whimpered. *"You* must."

In what? From where? The Bone Garden was surely meant to do exactly what it was doing now, sapping will, instilling dread, making Rhona wonder why she had ever thought to come here. Why should she be so privileged as to speak with the dead, with the many souls for whom she, Alerion, Mirkvahíl, and so many others were responsible for sentencing to this awful place?

She started at a tug on her hand. Looked down and saw the spirit of a young girl. Realized it was pulling not on her hand but on her *illum.* *"Please,"* it groaned, siphoning more of Rhona's illum. *"I...I am so...hungryyyyy..."*

Rhona tore her arm away. The spirit fell to mist with a rasp; more manifested in its wake. Silhouettes with stark white eyes and the slightest hints of facial features. Rhona ran. They followed. She sprinted blindly, purpose momentarily quelled in favor of safety, solitude, anywhere these things couldn't find her.

This must be what it feels like, what it looks like when guilt manifests, she thought, pushing back tears. Ghosts of yore, harbingers of sorrow, bannermen for a lady of woe. *They* were her legacy, and what an awful thing that was.

She stopped, turned to face the past. The spirits encircled her. They stood staring, little more than incorporeal effigies. What were they doing? What were they waiting for? Rhona opened her mouth—to say...what? To *ask* what?

"I was a farmer," said one.

"I was a nursemaid," said a second.

"We all of us were something to someone," said a third, brighter-eyed than the rest. It approached Rhona, stopping just a foot or two away, boring into her with a full-moon stare.

"You stripped us of our futures. You mistook subjugation for harmony, mistook individuality and freedom of speech for sedition. You whom we adored, whom we looked to for guidance. You are a lie."

Rhona swallowed. The words stung more than she had ever thought they could. "Is this why I have come? Is this—are *you* what I was meant to find?" She felt another tug on her illum. It was greater than the first and this time Rhona did not flee. Despite Fiel's frantic pleas she stood her ground, watching her illum leave her flesh in wispy, luminescent threads.

Djen—Mother Woe said the Bone Garden is the birthplace of clarity. Rhona faltered, dropped to one knee as the garden waxed and waned. *What...* Images flashed across her mind. They were little more than swirls of color. *What...am I... supposed to find...? Who—*

Who.

The wind howled and a shadow reared up before Rhona, more monstrous than anything she had ever seen. Her vision steadied, she went cold. Never before had she felt such dread. Lithe and winged, an orb of brilliant light where once a face had been or should have been. It plucked her from the earth with ease and held her to the blackened sky.

I will break you, it hissed, and its words were like the sea crashing against rock. *I will break you a thousand times. You are false. You are ruin.* A portion of the faceless orb dilated to reveal a maw, a pit of absolute and utter emptiness. *You are mine.*

Rhona wailed.

She fell.

———

RHONA BOLTED UPRIGHT from the grass with a gasp. Before her stood the Lost Tree. Beside her, a familiar figure.

"I should like to tell you it gets easier," Equilibrium said. "So much of me wishes I could—but that would be a lie. Nothing will *ever* be easy for you. You saw to that long ago, my dear friend."

Long ago. It was a phrase of such simplicity, yet the way Equilibrium said it told her there was a deeper meaning. Rhona could feel it in every fiber of her being and it made her cold. If she could only see behind the curtain of it all...

"Before this I was somewhere else," Rhona said. "The Bone Garden. And before that, with Mother Woe—with Djen, a name she claimed she hadn't used in centuries." Her brow furrowed. "I think I've lost all sense of time. All sense of...everything."

"On the contrary," Equilibrium said. "You are regaining sense. Fantasies and falsities, memories and dreams—all have brought you to this point. Your existence is a parable of utmost import. It will shape the future of your world."

Rhona's frown persisted. "What does that mean? Mother

Woe said the same thing, my existence being a parable." She punched the grass and growled. If she could only see what she was being pointed toward!

She blinked and Equilibrium was gone. Snow fell; the meadow was a blanket of white through which the Lost Tree rose. A familiar figure stood beneath its branches, staring directly at Rhona. She knew that white-eyed gaze intimately and stood, approaching hesitantly, trembling not from the cold but from the confusion of it all.

"Djen?"

"Memory is a complex thing," Djen said, walking to meet Rhona.

A ragged sigh escaped Rhona's lips. "Is...is that all this is? Is that all *you* are, here?"

Djen shrugged. "I...am many things everywhere."

"I just..." Rhona reached for Djen's hands, held them tightly. "I feel so lost."

"Such profound guilt has a way of doing that," Djen said sadly. "Just as power and authority dull one's sense of morality. One's compassion. Do you see the irony of it all?" She pulled Rhona to her, kissed her deeply. "The taste of regret is strong."

Rhona pulled back, tugged herself from Djen's grasp. Mother Woe stood staring back.

"*Hell is a place of one's own making,*" Mother Woe said, holding her arms out to the side. "*And the irony? In seeking to create utopia you did the exact opposite, you and Varésh Lúm-*

talé alike. No perfect world—only entropy. Only the beginning of the end."

The meadow darkened, melting away in rivulets to reveal the Bone Garden. Rhona's vision waxed and waned. Her equilibrium fluctuated violently. Had she ever left this place? Had she ever actually spoken to Equilibrium, to Djen, or had everything been a lie? She fell to the ground. All around her spirits moaned, tugging on her illum.

"As I said..." Mother Woe knelt beside Rhona, leaned in. Her breath was cold and sharp against Rhona's ear. *"I will break you."*

Then—

———

VELA and her prisoner were halfway through the woods.

It was cold here where the sun was silent, where the world was quieter still. Her mind was chaos. Why had her village chosen Vela for a task so horrible as this? How could they reasonably expect her to spill the blood of the woman she had known since childhood? The questions were rhetorical—Vela *knew* the answers.

"Are you going to kill me?" asked Djorev for what felt like the millionth time.

Vela was silent. How was she to answer? Sacrificing Djorev would keep their village and the land of Jémoon safe; it was Vela's duty as a Walker. But it would break her heart.

To sacrifice Djorev was to betray their friendship. Vela tightened her grip on Djorev's leash, cursing *alf elo nor*. The Jémoon tenet decreeing *one for all* was a wretched thing.

"Are you ever going to answer me?"

"I don't know," Vela said finally.

"I wouldn't blame you if you did," said Djorev. "I'm spellscarred."

The word stung every time Djorev used it.

Curse you, Vela thought of the Raven, the deity warding Jémoon. *This is your fault.*

"You shouldn't blaspheme so loudly," said Djorev. "It's only going to make this worse."

Vela stopped and wheeled around. Djorev's stark white eyes gazed back from the depths of her hood. "How could this get any worse? Why should I care if the Raven hears what I say? It's that overgrown bird's fault you're tied to this leash. If it had done its duty to Jémoon and kept the Vulture quelled, you wouldn't be infected by wild Dusk."

"But the Raven didn't, and I am," said Djorev. "Now here we are in a dark forest, arguing as the wolves descend." Vela gave her a questioning look. "I heard them a mile back. Except for the obvious stigma, being spellscarred isn't *all* bad."

Vela drew her dagger, wondering how close the wolves were. "I wish you would take this a bit more seriously."

Djorev grinned. "Afraid the severity's slipped my mind?" She snapped her fingers and her bonds and tether turned to ash. "Hmm. Wonder what that little magic trick cost..."

Vela groaned. She didn't want to think about it. The price of a spellscarred's power was terribly unpredictable and unpredictably terrible. It was a small part of why Vela made no move to apprehend Djorev. The bigger part was *because* it was Djorev—Vela trusted her to stick by her side regardless of the circumstances.

"About four or five wolves half a mile behind us." Djorev grabbed Vela's hand and yanked her along. A bead of light bloomed overhead and proceeded to illuminate their way as they fled.

"We could take the wolves," said Vela.

"Or we could save our strength and run," said Djorev, and that really meant, "Or we could not risk me blowing us up."

Vela decided it was the right call.

———

THE TREES HAD THINNED by the time they stopped running.

Vela doubled over to catch her breath. Djorev leaned against a tree, singing softly, indiscernibly. How long had they fled? How long ago had they left the village? Had the sun still been up or had it been night?

"I wonder if I could kill the Vulture," Djorev said. "I wield what wrought it, after all."

Vela rose to her full height and frowned. "More likely than not, you would destroy Jémoon if you tried. Or, at the very least, yourself, and then what would I do?"

Djorev shrugged and pulled her cloak a bit tighter. "Find another spellscarred to love?"

That stung more than the word spellscarred did. Vela swallowed her rage and the lump in her throat. "Doubtful."

There was a long, cricket-filled silence between them.

"This is a really shit situation," said Djorev with a noticeable quiver in her words. Such evident fear was rare in her. It was often times masked by grins and forced jokes, much as she had been doing ever since they had set out on this wretched task.

"Djorev..." Vela pulled her into her arms and held her tight.

"What if I promised not to use my power?" Djorev whispered. "Could I go back? Could things go back to the way they were?"

Vela knew the answer. Village law was strict. To be spellscarred was to be a sacrifice, and sacrifices kept the Raven strong. The way Walkers saw it, bleeding a spellscarred dry took strength from the Vulture, especially if it was true the spellscarred were manifestations of the Vulture. She buried her face in Djorev's hood and sighed.

"Are you thirsty?" Djorev asked.

Vela chuckled softly. "Terribly." She pulled away from Djorev and knelt by the tree, digging half a foot into the earth. She pricked her finger with the tip of her dagger, intoning, "*Alf elo nor*," as the blood dripped onto the roots and into the dirt. In return, the tree presented them with the means to quench their thirst. As it was in life, alf elo nor was the way of things in the woods.

"How far from the Nohl Waypoint do you think we are?" Djorev asked when they had finished.

"A day or two," said Vela. "Hopefully not longer." The Raven only came to the shrine once a month, and a missed sacrifice meant further catastrophe. The Vulture's strength would grow, the Raven's would wane. Rivers would dry up. Game would grow sparse. Plagues would spread and people would starve.

Vela stood and helped Djorev to her feet. "Come on. We can sleep when the longest yawns come."

———

IT WAS STILL DARK when those yawns came, but the darkness was peppered with stars as Vela and Djorev emerged from the woods. Before them stretched a meadow; the forest path had turned from dirt to a mottling of stones. A gentle breeze tousled the reeds and a perfume of vanilla and honey permeated the air. Vela breathed it in with a contented sigh. It had been at least a year since she had smelled it; it relaxed her mind.

She looked at Djorev, who beckoned to her from the grass.

"Promise I won't accidentally blow you up with a snore," said Djorev with a weary smile.

Vela chuckled and joined Djorev, pressing against her for warmth. She closed her eyes and sighed. The world could wait for a night.

———

VELA STARED AT the oak tree and she knew this was a dream. The tree was beautiful in its gnarled and twisted way, its white leaves like suspended snow. She had dreamt it many times before, though she could not say why. As she had the oak tree, she had dreamt this meadow too, its grass a golden sea.

The Raven stood before the tree. It was larger than a horse, with feathers dark as night and eyes like mid-month moons. Beside the Raven stood a man with feathered wings and charcoal eyes. He was called Varésh and she had dreamt him many times before.

"Child, you return." He took her in his arms. He was warm and smelled of cold nights and campfire smoke.

"I do not know why." Vela sighed into his chest.

"Don't you?" Varésh asked, and he pulled away to look her in the eyes.

She had seen that stare before, soft and knowing all at once. "I am scared."

"Tell me," said Varésh. "Tell me of your fear."

Vela eyed the Raven. Its wings leaked gossamer threads of Dusk. The meadow wilted and the oak tree fell to ashen rot.

The Raven met her gaze before it too was ravaged. In its wake a single night-black talon lay.

"Failure," said Varésh. "I am very intimate with failure."

"How do you face it?" Vela asked. "How do you face the fear of failure when your own morality holds you back?" Tears stung her eyes. "I never asked to Walk. I never asked to sacrifice my friend."

"And yet you know you must." He kissed her forehead. "Lest you doom Jémoon to rot."

"*Alf elo nor,*" she whispered, and the world dissolved.

———

VELA WALKED with heavy legs and a crick in her neck. She had slept little the previous night and the dream still clung to her like a shawl, light but heavy enough to perceive. Her conscience was compromised and it put the people of Jémoon at risk. What was she to do?

You know, a side of her hissed.

It is not right, another argued. *It is not fair.*

Life is not meant to be, the first side said. *Everything dies; every soul is alf elo nor.*

And yet the notion of taking a life— Djorev's life—still felt wrong; it made her stomach churn. She balled her hands into fists and growled to herself. Why could they not simply pray to the Raven? Why could it not subsist simply on praise?

For the same reason courtship is more than handwritten

letters and words, said the voice in her head. *Action says more than a word could ever convey.*

In most cases.

What would you have me do? Vela asked of nothing in particular.

Djorev was silent as they walked, and that was probably for the best.

———

THE EARLY MORNING sun beat down upon them, tempered by a mottling of clouds. Save a trio of snowjays, Vela and Djorev were alone. In a way it was nice. To be alone in the wilds was something Vela had dreamt of for years. The reflexive nature of home had grown to be gratingly dull.

But it was harrowing, too. Save Djorev, she was alone with a knife, her fears, and her thoughts—and that was a dangerous thing. The fate of Jémoon rested on her shoulders, and Vela was not sure it was a weight she could bear.

They kept on. The clouds devoured the sun and a gentle breeze swept across the meadow, tousling her hair. Even though they were alone Vela could not help feeling as though their steps were being watched. Spirits lurked in the plains, but they were rare and mostly kept to themselves.

Perhaps a jétjune, she thought. The fox-like sprites were notoriously drawn to Walkers.

Or maybe the feeling was nothing at all. Djorev had yet to notice anything, and her senses were greater than Vela's.

At length they came to a ruin through which a river ran south. It was the village of Yahn, marked by a crumbling tower of stone. Yahn was the precursor to Nohl, or had been at least. Now it was dead and guarding the forest passage to Nohl.

"Cheery," Djorev said.

"It was beautiful once," said Vela. "Or so I have read."

She walked the weed-covered streets in a daze, Djorev haunting her steps like a silent wraith. How long had it been since Yahn stood whole? No one could seem to recall. For that, Vela was sad. How many names had been lost to time, never whispered again? The wild Dusk did terrible things and the very thought of Yahn's desolation filled her with fear. A cold sweat blossomed on her brow. Was this what fate had in store for her village if she failed to bleed Djen dry at the shrine?

They came to the village square. Djorev sat, massaging her legs while Vela wandered. Just north of the square was the tower. Vela approached it and ran her hand along the weathered white stone. She felt a connection, an attachment to Yahn born of study, stories, and dreams. So many times she had climbed to the top of this tower, so many times she had run through these streets chasing children or dogs.

She ducked beneath its crumbling archway. Inside it smelled collectively of dust and wet earth, of history. Even now, Vela could make out the remnants of inlays depicting the Raven, wide-winged and dark. She bowed her head to the image. It was a reflex born of reverent superstition, though this time it was meant as an apology for the previous night's blasphemy. Outwardly, she placed the brunt of the blame on the Raven, but in her heart she knew the Walkers of yore were equally to blame with their belated offerings. As important as alf elo nor was, the Jémoon tenet nor elo alf—all for one—was equally as significant.

"Want to have a deeper look?"

Vela started. "Must you always be so silent with your steps?"

Djorev poked Vela in the small of her back. "Is that a yes?"

"So long as we don't disturb anything."

"If we do, I shall be the first to know," said Djorev, tapping her skull. "Come on."

The tower bloomed with strange pastel light the deeper in they went. It was peaceful and brought a bit of majesty to a place ruled by utter desolation. How beautiful the tower must have been in Yahn's heyday, filled with scholars and mages dedicated to the wellbeing of Jémoon.

"I had a dream about Yahn last night," said Djorev. "At least, I think it was Yahn."

Vela had dreamt as well, though hers had be decidedly different. "I once read dreams are sometimes more than dreams." She wasn't sure how much stock she put in such a notion but it was fascinating to think about nonetheless. "What did you see in yours?"

"Yahn as it once had been." Djorev pulled her hood back. The extent of her spellscarred transformation was jarring even now. Pale flesh, cracked and mottled; stark white eyes encapsulated by dark circles. "You're staring again."

Vela averted her gaze. "Sorry."

"At least I know you aren't judging me for it," said Djorev. "Yahn was a garden once, at least in my dream. I saw colors I couldn't put names to. It was beautiful. *Everyone* was beautiful. And there were duskeels that swam through the sky, and dawneels."

No one ever talked about the Dawn, the inverse of the Dusk, for the simple reason it was little more than a myth. If the energy existed none could say when, not for certain. And if the Raven of Jémoon had ever wielded such a force it had all but forgotten how.

"I wish I could see what you see," Vela said. Her dreams of Yahn were different but beautiful in their own way. Still, she longed for something to share with Djorev besides this terrible journey.

"Maybe someday you will." Djorev took her hand and they pressed on.

The ruin grew more profound as they ascended a winding stairway. Sunlight streamed through cracks and holes in the wall. Several times the stairway itself threatened to collapse. Strangest of all was the dark membrane-like substance mottling the wall for as high as Vela could stare.

"What do you suppose this is?"

"Some form of Dusk." There was dark certainty in Djorev's reply, and the black mottling on her flesh seemed to react to the membrane, reshaping itself to various patterns as if ink dripped on parchment.

"We should leave," said Vela as they reached the second-floor landing. The Dusk's presence was prominent here. Gossamer threads twirled and twisted from the membrane, flittering through the air. It made Vela's skin crawl, made her forehead slick with cold sweat. "Djorev?"

"It's harmless." Djorev held her hand out to the wispy strands of Dusk and they came to her, coiling through her splayed fingers and up her arm. "Duskeels, see?"

And Vela *could*. Nearly indiscernible were a pair of white dots she suspected were eyes.

"I think this tower is their nest," Djorev said. "This stuff on the walls."

"What was your skin reacting to?"

Djorev shrugged. "Close proximity to anything made of Dusk? A lot of this spellscarred stuff I haven't figured out yet." She brought her arm before her eyes, smiling at the duskeel, chuckling as the creature mewed. "Gentle little things, these eels."

Her eye twitched and she cocked her head. "Did you hear that?"

"No." Vela tried to follow Djorev's gaze.

"Sounded like...crying, from the floor above." Djorev started up the stairs at a vigilant pace, Vela trailing with her dagger drawn.

Leave it to Djorev to find a ghost, she thought, though she wasn't entirely sure *what* Djorev had heard. It was certainly possible the tower was occupied by a hermit or a lost traveler, or that a jétjune was playing tricks as their kind were wont to do. Hopefully it wasn't anything more.

The third floor was little more than a writhing mass of Dusk, myriad eels flittering about. Djorev walked with certainty. Coldness emanated from her; in fact, Vela could discern a faint aura about her person—what was it?

"Are you all right, Djorev? You're glowing..."

Djorev said nothing as they wound deeper. Eels parted before her like grass in a breeze. Whether in reverence or fear, Vela was not certain. She *was* certain that she was a bit fearful of Djorev, of whatever they were searching for.

What a pathetic way to fail that would be. The very thought of dying here just a day removed from their village filled Vela with shame, enough she could hardly keep from snorting at the notion.

"Stop."

Vela nearly bumped into Djorev. Before them a worn wooden door stood ajar. Beyond the door, darkness, peppered with flittering motes of light. Here, at the threshold of uncertainty, Vela finally heard it—displaced crying, as if it existed on two planes at once.

"After me, I suppose," Djorev murmured. She pushed past the door and into the room.

Vela followed suit and the dreamlike attachment returned. There was an air of familiarity about this room and its inlayed floor, its meadow view and the figure standing several feet away. A woman garbed in white with a mane of fire-red hair. Behind her stood a tree, *the tree* from Vela's dream and—

Vela blinked. The room had dissolved; there was only a meadow, the woman, and the tree.

"So long," the woman murmured, looking Vela. "So long I have waited." Her yellow eyes were a mixture of fear and relief. She approached Vela and took her hands. "Thank the Raven you have come."

What is this? Where is Djorev? What was going on?

Vela tried to pull away but the woman's grasp was firm.

"Please, take me from this awful place." The woman's eyes were wet with desperation.

"Tell me who you are." Everything about this felt wrong.

"Please! Before it comes!" the woman cried.

Vela tried to pull away, again to no avail. "Before *what* comes? What is going on?"

A shriek ripped through the meadow. The grass wilted beneath the horrible sound and the tree's leaves turned to ash, falling from the branches like a pathetic snow. The woman screamed, falling to her knees, hands pressed to her ears.

"It comes! It comes! The Vulture!"

A great shadow darkened the meadow. Vela's hair stood on end, goosepimples rippled across her arms and neck. She looked to the sky as the shape came back around, long-necked and black with six great wings trailing into smoke. The Vulture screeched and Vela bled from her eyes, nose, and ears. She fell to the grass, writhing, watching as the horrible shadow swooped and took the woman in its beak. With a snap it halved her and the remnants fell to the ground with a thud.

Vela forced herself to stand; her legs trembled terribly as she approached the remains.

But there was nothing save swirls of smoke.

She started at a flap of wings and whisper in her ear and spun around.

Gasped as Djorev pulled a jagged blade from her chest with a squelch.

"So long I waited," she whispered as Vela spat blood, as the meadow waxed and waned. She pulled Vela close so their noses were just inches apart. "So long." Her bright eyes were narrowed, a swirl of triumph and emptiness. "Alf elo nor. Nor elo alf."

"DREAMS ARE SOMETIMES MORE THAN DREAMS," said Varésh. "One might choose to think of them as cries from the subconscious. But you already know that, of course. Tell me, child—save failure, what do your dreams bespeak?"

"Failure is all my dreams suggest," said Vela. She gestured at the oak tree and its leaves like winter snow. "So many times I have seen this wilt. So many times I have seen this meadow die." She wrapped her arms around herself, trembling. "And this time I saw it—the Vulture. I saw it kill. I saw its pestilent influence unbounded all because I failed my Walk. And..."—Vela shuddered—"I think the Vulture was *her*—Djorev. She stabbed me, Varésh."

"Peculiar things, these dreams we dream." Varésh stretched his great wings then furled them like a cloak. "Peculiar more, the things of which we dream."

Vela frowned. "What do you mean?"

Varésh reached forward, cupping her cheek. "You know well what I mean." His eyes bore into hers and Vela felt a fog dissolving from her mind. "There are no such things as Ravens and Walks."

———

"GLAD TO SEE YOU UP. Been out cold for a week."

Anja blinked. Remnants of a dream clung to her like mist and her head ached something fierce. A gray-eyed man with a hawkish face and dark hair pulled back behind his ears stared down at her. He wore a warm smile.

Anja returned it with a weary one of her own. "Varésh."

He leaned in and kissed her forehead. "How are you feeling?"

"Dazed." She wasn't sure if that was the proper word but it fit for the time being. "Like I drank far too much at the tavern. So many weird dreams... You were there and..." Anja frowned. "So was Djal Shy'eth."

"I would expect nothing less from the Dreamweaver who did this to you," said Varésh. "Quite a nasty reputation and a particular distaste for you. Not fond of being locked away in Misten Fahg either, it seems."

"Don't really blame her for that," said Anja. Misten Fahg, renowned tower college of magi, was an absolute lie. A beautiful lie but a lie nonetheless. It was a prison, the magi its guards.

She sat up and pushed a few loose strands of hair out of her face. She could see the moon out the window at the far end of the room, brilliant and full, boring into her like a knowing eye. Bits and pieces of her dream waltzed across her mind, dissolving as quickly as they appeared. What a strange thing it had been.

"Anything interesting happen while I was out?" Anja asked.

Varésh's expression darkened. "A day after your encounter with Djal something came out of the Old Wood."

Names and words carried weight. Some were said to have true power. It was this very belief, this very superstition, that kept most from calling the Old Wood by its given name, Hang-Dead Forest.

"What was it?" Anja asked.

"Hungry. A shadow of a man."

Had this shadow come from anywhere else, Anja would have simply rolled her eyes. But things emerging from Hang-Dead Forest were cause for concern, rare as they were. The last time—and many years before Anja's birth—a man had come to the village Nohl in the dark of night. When the sun rose the following morning the village was dead and the man was gone. All that remained were myriad corpses, rotted and swaddled in smoke.

"Any idea where it might have gone?"

Varésh was silent. His brow was etched with worry.

Anja frowned. "Out with it."

"Here," Varésh said. "It came here. You and I are the only ones left."

Anja looked him in the eyes. "What do you mean, we're the only ones left?"

"Everyone else in Misten Fahg is dead," Varésh said. "Magi, acolytes, prisoners, the whole lot. Dead and gone, and soon the college will be too. Whatever this shadow man is, its presence is deteriorating the structure. We're only alive, you and I, because I've kept this room warded the last week." He heaved a sigh and wiped his brow. "Quite exhausting."

Great. Was it wrong to wish she were still stuck in her dream? At least the scenery had been nice. Anja took a deep breath to compose herself, to reconnect with her illum and mirkúr, the innate power of magi. The energies returned to her gradually and she felt comfortably cold and warm all at once.

"Maybe you should have a rest," she said to Varésh.

"Or," he said, "maybe we should flee."

Anja frowned. "And leave this thing to eat the rest of Misten Fahg?"

"Precisely that." Varésh chuckled wryly. "It's not as if we can stop it here. The entire college of magi is dead. What chance do the two of us stand?"

He had a point. Somehow, he always had a point.

"Flee to where?" Anja asked.

"Below."

Gods, but she hated the finality of his tone. Below wasn't just *below.* It was a very specific below: Banerowos, the city under Misten Fahg, the vast ruin from which the college drew its power.

"Pray tell, what good would fleeing to Banerowos do us?"

"I know what lurks within," Varésh said. "In the very bowels of its ruin. I know what sleeps, I know how to awaken it, and I think it will help."

"This sounds like a horrible decision," said Anja. Misten Fahg shook and a grating shriek ripped through the otherwise silent night. "But I suppose it beats the alternatives." She slipped out of bed, garbed as she had been the day she'd fought Djal. "Drop the wards and lead the way."

———

FOR THE FIRST time in all her years at Misten Fahg, Anja was glad her room had been on the second floor of the tower. She stood in the hallway, looking up at the night sky and the massive chunks of stone. They were suspended and floating through the air, as if trapped in time. Tendrils of shadow trailed in their wake. Whatever this thing from Hang-Dead Forest was, it was terribly powerful. As she followed Varésh down the remnants of the stairs it occurred to her they had no idea where in Misten Fahg it was lurking. The notion made her spine tingle.

Varésh, tired as he had claimed to be, walked with a bounce to his step. Dropping the wards and reclaiming the illum he'd used to scrawl them seemed to have roused him a bit. For that, Anja was glad. She had no idea how to get to wherever in Banerowos they were headed, and two against one were much better odds, slim as they already were, should they run into the shadow.

"All the light in Misten Fahg is gone," she remarked.

"The shadow must have eaten the rest of the illum," Varésh said.

So *that* was what he'd meant by 'hungry.' What name,

what word must have been invoked for a thing of such terrible power to have emerged from Hang-Dead Forest?

"Do you think there's any correlation between this shadow and the man who brought the plague to Nohl?" Anja asked.

Varésh shrugged. "Could be. But it's hard to know for sure."

The stairway leveled out into a large, circular vestibule. Threads of shadow flittered through the air. Anja swore they were whispering to her in a language she could not understand. She ignored the cold tickling in her ears as best she could, focusing on floor beneath their feet and the ruined inlay of the Raven God. It reminded her of the tower in her dream, of the dreams within her dreams—a winged Varésh and a Raven larger than a horse. Gods, but what the hell had Djal done to her?

"Do you think *all* the prisoners are dead?" she asked. Her thoughts were fixed on Djal, now, and she couldn't push the Dreamweaver from her mind.

"I'm not sure."

That meant there was a small chance they might find Djal.

And why would I want to do that? Anja cursed herself for having such a thought.

Answers, said a voice in her head.

What?

About your dream, the voice clarified. *Answers about the shadow. Who's to say she didn't call this thing here?*

You have a point, Anja conceded, *but recall Djal, mad as she is, has never been one for absolute destruction of life. She's never so much as killed a fly.*

Anja had known Djal for years; there was history between them, more than she cared to let Varésh and anyone else know about. She hadn't thought about their years together, their years as friends in a long time. The pain was still too much, her heart was raw even now.

They withdrew from the interior of Misten Fahg, headed south across the grounds. These too were dead. Trees were bare and twisted. Effigies were little more than rubble. As had been the case inside the tower, debris floated through the air, trailed by gossamer strands of smoke. It was reasonable to think the village of Nohl, which stood at the base of Misten Fahg, had once more succumbed to the destructive power of this thing from Hang-Dead Forest. History was wicked that way.

The desolation grew more profound the closer they drew to the archway leading into Banerowos. The Misten Fahg grounds were little more than shadowlands. Varésh conjured an illum wisp to light their way, but even it was little match for the darkness encircling them; within seconds the light was devoured.

"Can we even activate the archway?" Anja asked. "If this

darkness so quickly consumes light are the glyphs in the pillars going to hold their illum?"

They stopped before the archway, grand and intricately wrought. It was older than Misten Fahg itself, a relic from the days of Banerowos. Its connection to the dead city was the only reason it stood, unsullied by the hungering darkness.

Varésh took a deep breath. He placed his hands atop the glyphs in the right-side column; Anja did so on the left. "Ready?"

She nodded. Illum flowed through her body, warm and welcoming against the pervasive blackness of the world. Keeping the channel was difficult, strenuous, but Anja had expected it to be. Illumination left her fingertips in streams, twisting, conforming to the glyphs' designs. She held her breath, willing more of the energy into the pillars as the darkness—wild mirkúr, she'd decided—tried to wrest the light away.

"Why struggle?" something whispered in her mind. It was cold and serpentine. "Why fight when the simpler thing, the easier thing, is to relent? What are you running from? What do you seek?"

Anja screamed as the whisper's frigidity consumed her. She poured every ounce of illum she had into the glyphwork, and the archway exploded with light. A majestic ruin rippled into view. Without a second thought she grabbed Varésh and they leapt across the threshold.

IT WAS dusk and the meadow smelled of fresh rain.

The oak tree bore no leaves for it was that time of year. Anja leaned against its trunk, the grass soft against her legs and feet. Djal sat beside her, chewing on a reed, and before them stood Varésh, head tilted high, wings spread wide in all their midnight glory as he basked in the warmth of the setting sun.

The Raven soared above them, gentle strands of shadow streaming in its wake. The great bird swooped down into the grass. It landed and approached Anja, nuzzling her with its beak. She had found the largest things were often times the gentlest and the Raven was no different.

"I heard something once," said Djal, looking at Anja.

"You've heard a lot of things."

"Yes, but nothing so profound as this—dreams are sometimes more than dreams."

"Profound, yes, but silly, too," said Anja. "Dreams are nothing more."

Djal tossed her reed away. "According to whom?"

"Everyone."

Djal crossed her arms. "Everyone, hmm?"

Anja nodded.

"And how do they know this for a fact?"

"Because it's always been a fact," said Anja. "What else would dreams be?"

"Cries from our subconscious," said Djal. She cupped Anja's cheek. "This is not the first time I have died."

She wilted, turned to ash as easily as parchment in a flame.

———

Sunlight greeted Yora's eyes and she shut them immediately. Her body ached horribly, her mind more so. She knew exactly what had happened and it frightened her. The blackouts were coming with increasing frequency—they had been since that night in Hang-Dead Forest. Whatever she had encountered there had done something to her physiology; she was losing control over her Dusk and Dawn.

"There you are! I've been scouring Banerowos for hours."

Yora opened her eyes at the voice. "Djema."

"You had me worried sick," said Djema, helping Yora to her feet. She brushed Yora's cheek. "It happened again, didn't it?"

Yora nodded wearily.

Djema took her hands. "You're trembling. Gods, what did this thing do to you?"

"I wish I knew." So many lucid dreams. An endless string of phantasmagoria stacked within each other. Was this another one? "This is going to sound crazy, but...I don't even know if I'm dreaming or awake right now, Djema."

Djema pulled her into a firm embrace. "You are most certainly awake right now."

"That sounds like something a player in a dream would say," whispered Yora. "Something I would *make* them say to maintain the illusion of truth." She shuddered. "So many false realities..."

"Have you spoken to anyone else about this?" Djema asked. "Any of the other Ravens?"

"No." Yora knew by look on Djema's face she should have told her, should have told Varésh. They were the keepers and guardians of Jémoon. If they were to fall then Jémoon would be lost to the wild Dusk.

"You need to. Today," said Djema. "Now, even. The wild Dusk is growing stronger, hungrier, and if even one of us is compromised it could very well spell the end of Jémoon." Her expression softened; her white eyes were glossy. "We have lost so much already."

So many cities, towns, and villages, devoured by the wild Dusk. Yora had lost track of the death toll. Worst of all was the fact she and the rest of the Ravens still had yet to uncover just how the Dusk had gone rogue. For centuries they had kept it tempered without issue, and for centuries they had used the converse powers of Dusk and Dawn to shape the land of Jémoon. What had gone wrong?

"Are you able to fly?" Djema asked, unfurling her wings.

Yora's own ached horribly. She could barely keep them furled. "I doubt it."

"I suppose a walk might help." Djema took her hand and they started through the barren streets of Banerowos. Even now the emptiness was eerie; only months ago the streets had been routinely filled with people going about their days. Now they all kept to their homes and the relative safety provided by their wards. Their fear was palpable and it broke Yora's heart, especially because she felt, *knew* she was partly responsible. What kind of Raven was she if should could not help her brethren protect their people from the encroaching end?

"It's so easy to forget how beautiful this place is," Djema murmured. "The cost of fighting to survive, I suppose. I'm scared, Yora. Things are getting worse. I know you've noticed."

Yora had, but for the life of her could not remember *how* they had gotten worse. It was hard to keep track of it all when she could barely keep track of herself.

"And yet the struggle perseveres."

Yora went cold at the voice in her head. It was the very same she had heard in her dream.

"What do you fear? Why not relent?" it hissed. *"Why not let the veil part?"*

You aren't real, Yora thought.

The voice chuckled. *"Aren't I? I am infinite. Reliably and consistently present."*

Yora swallowed. *Am I going mad?*

"A sane question." Yora couldn't tell if the voice was serious or if it was mocking her. *"What do you think?"*

I think, Yora replied, *I understand absolutely nothing anymore.*

"*Sometimes we need to start from scratch in order to fully comprehend what we are dealing with,*" it said. "*As you have heard so many times before, dreams are sometimes more than dreams. There is truth to be found in madness. And regardless of whatever opinions of me you have already formed, know I am here to help you. We are, after all, twins of a sort.*"

Somehow that put Yora at ease. Not completely, but enough she could focus on the spires of the Raven's Perch rising up in the distant center of Banerowos. She let go of Djema's hand and rolled her shoulders. She stretched her wings, painful as it was, and gave a great flap. The streets grew smaller with every passing second as she ascended, Djema following in her wake as they soared over Banerowos and made for the Perch.

———

"You should have informed us immediately," said Varésh. His eyes flashed angrily in the sunlight pouring into the chamber. "We can ill afford to be compromised when the perseverance of Jémoon depends upon us."

Yora made no attempt to argue. He was right.

"Did you know of this?" Varésh asked Djema.

"Not until earlier today," she said. "Have we found any

trace of whatever came out of Hang-Dead Forest? Perhaps *it* might be the key curing Yora's ailment."

"No. Orjem has yet to return," said Varésh, "and that could mean anything."

Yora wasn't even aware Orjem had left. "Where did he go?"

Varésh and Djema frowned.

"The lands surrounding the forest," Varésh said. "You were present when he left. *You* suggested we send a party to investigate the ruins at its center."

"Perhaps we should send another to search for Orjem," Yora said. Her flesh had turned to goosepimples at Varésh's revelation. "Or maybe..." She sighed and rubbed the bridge of her nose. "Is there anything else I should know? Anything I might have forgotten?"

Djema and Varésh looked at each other.

"Why flee?"

The sunlight went silent.

"What do you fear?"

Their flesh paled and cracked, peeled away to reveal mottlings of Dusk.

"Te Mirkvahíl!"

Yora screamed. She turned and leapt from the chamber window, taking flight over the Dusk-constricted corpse of Banerowos. Tendrils and tentacles of shadow felled the once majestic city, turned its streets black and devoured every bit of illumination for as far as Yora could see.

"Te Mirkvahíl." The voice was solid, near—it had escaped her mind. Her echo rose up to meet her. She gripped Yora by the throat and they hurtled toward the streets. "WHAT. DO. YOU. FEAR?"

———

RHONA WAS ALONE beneath the oak tree. It was night and the stars were asleep; the moon too refused to shine.

"And here we are." Her echo manifested in a swirl of smoke. "Again. You cannot flee forever. Your vultures will inevitably prevail. You will discover the truth buried in all of this madness. Trust me—I have seen it many times before." It knelt and looked Rhona in the eyes. "Hell is a place of our own making. If you continue down this path, you'll not come out alive."

Tears trickled down Rhona's cheeks. "You think I want this? To be stuck in these dreams, these horrible falsities?"

Her echo smiled sadly. "If you didn't, you would have let the truth find you. But instead you run. Run as you have run for years, dreaming your dreams, taking name after name. Part of it is fear, part of it is guilt, shame. But all of it, Te Mirkvahíl? All of it is self-inflicted penance."

"For what?" Rhona asked. "What could I have done to wish this...this madness on myself?"

Her echo stood and offered its hand. "Why not stand and see?"

A white portal swirled into existence several yards from the tree. Through it Rhona saw herself in the Bone Garden, that thing leering over her like—

"The Vulture," she whispered, taking her echo's hand.

"Indeed," her echo said.

It locked eyes with her again. Rhona felt cold, sick like she never had before. She started for the portal.

"Wake up," a distant voice said. *"Wake up."*

"WAKE UP."

"WAKE UP."

WAKE. UP!

———

You WAKE, now, wide-eyed, ragged-winged and filched of light. What a sorry creature at my feet. A flightless bird, an introspective liar. A glutton for eternal penance. Lo, she whimpers. Lo, she shuts her eyes to the truth—the woebegotten land beneath the tower high. Lo, the Phoenix Mirkvahíl whispers:

"Oh gods...what have I done?"

Perception is fickle, dangerously so. Often times we see things as we wish they were; we see ourselves as something we are not. We dream to run from what we fear—but the truth is never far behind. The guilt will always call you back. Welcome, Mirkvahíl, to the ruin of your world.

10

LUMINÍL'S LAMENT

MIRKVAHÍL PUSHED HERSELF TO STAND; she could not. The atrophy kept her weighted to the ground, to the weathered stone atop the pinnacle of Banerowos, what was left of it at least. Before her stood Luminíl, flesh cracked and ruined as had been the case for Djen and Mother Woe, for Djorev and Djema. Mirkvahíl knew this was real. She knew she was finally awake, Luminíl's words echoing in her mind like a throng of buzzing flies.

"Look at you, Mirkvahíl." Luminíl's voice was bereft of its previous otherworldly depth. She knelt before Mirkvahíl, boring into her with a cold white stare, strands of platinum hair falling out from behind her ears. "Look at what you've done."

Mirkvahíl craned her neck as best she could. Banerowos was little more than a corpse of stone and snow, an amalgamation of every city she had seen in dreams. Somewhere north of here stood Hang-Dead Forest and the myriad murdered souls for whom she was to blame.

"Power corrupts," Luminíl said. "That is the way of it."

A ragged sigh escaped Mirkvahíl. "Parable." She held out a trembling, upturned palm. "This is what you meant when I met you as Mother Woe." Tears dripped down her cheeks. "My story, my existence..."

Luminíl nodded. Thus far she was less monstrous than she had been in Mirkvahíl's myriad dreams, both in mannerisms and appearance. There was a softness to her, a sadness, and it pained Mirkvahíl tremendously.

"I wonder how much of it all you truly remember," Luminíl said. "The Fall, and everything from which it grew. I'd venture little judging from your labyrinthine dreams. At the very least, some, though horrendously dissected and distorted."

She brushed a cold hand across Mirkvahíl's cheek, lingering for a half second before she pulled away. "Would that I could I would rewrite history and change this all." Her expression darkened. "I would change much."

Luminíl's words were calm, measured, but Mirkvahíl knew what the Vulture meant, and who was she to argue? She had done horrible things to Luminíl and her acolytes. "As would I," she whispered. She expected no sympathy from Luminíl. It just felt like the proper thing to say.

"I'm sorry." As did that.

"An apology..." Luminíl smiled wryly. "Were I you, I too would say the same, but expressed regret for your atrocities bears little weight a century and a half into ruin. Apologies will not remake the world. Apologies will not bring back the dead, nor will they mend my wounds."

Luminíl stood, and Mirkvahíl pushed herself to do the same a second time. She rose to her full height and stumbled forward into Luminíl like a newborn foal. The Vulture caught her, held her in her arms. For a moment, they stared into each other's eyes. For a moment, holding Luminíl and being held by her felt like a dream from which Mirkvahíl didn't want to wake. She clung to Luminíl, but the Vulture pulled away and Mirkvahíl fell to her knees, choking back tears.

"You'll gain no sympathy from me," said Luminíl. "You shame yourself, Mirkvahíl. Weeping and wallowing as if you've earned your tears." Shadow surged around her, enveloping Luminíl, shaping her into a lithe and monstrous silhouette with tattered wings and a glowing orb where once her face had been.

"I should end you," Luminíl hissed. In a twist of smoke she was before Mirkvahíl, taloned hand gripping her throat tight. "I should annihilate you for what you did to me, to Banerowos and Jémoon. I loved you more than anything—and you infected me, imprisoned me, and left me to rot. You destroyed everything."

Mirkvahíl clawed at Luminíl but the Vulture's grip held strong.

"I need you to see. I need you to remember, Mirkvahíl. I need you to remember as I rip your soul asunder. Hell is a place of one's own making, and I will send you back to walk yours for as long as you exist. No matter how many realities you dream, no matter how many different names you take, the guilt will always find you."

Mirkvahíl's vision waned. Planes of existence fluctuated manically.

"Abandon hope..."

———

Trees.

So many trees.

They whisper murderously.

———

Mirkvahíl shrieked.

———

So many trees. They call to you, whispering songs of yesteryears.

Rain. The heavens weep as you walk.

Tears touch your cheeks. Fear and desperation permeate your soul.

For Banerowos, you think. *For all Jémoon and Harmony.*

It pains you more than anything, that thought—but the worst is yet to come. So you walk and you listen to songs of the trees, listen to the madness pushing you along. Your illum showed you darkness not yet born. Your dreams of late serve only to cement your fear of encroaching desolation. They bring you here, to your favorite tree, the Lost Tree, to the girl beneath the tree.

I smile.

———

Illum leaked from Mirkvahíl. Through her flesh, through every orifice as Luminíl tugged ravenously on her soul, on her sanity, on her tether to this plane. She kicked feebly at the Vulture, cried out louder than her strength should have allowed.

"Relent, Mirkvahíl,

for I am the way into woe,

the way into the labyrinth eternal,

the way into Hell.

As Hang-Dead Forest whispered long ago,

abandon hope all ye who enter here."

———

I TAKE YOU IN MY ARMS, Mirkvahíl, as you join me beneath the tree. It has been a week since last I felt your touch. Tending to this world we three created takes its toll. You smell of honey and vanilla as you always do.

You kiss me.

I melt.

You pull away. Fear is present in your pitch-black eyes, in the galaxies they hold. I touch your cheek, you pull away. The forest sings and you furl your wings about yourself, a barricade, a barrier between your flesh and mine.

"Mirkvahíl?" I approach you, and I fall.

You stand your ground.

The sky darkens and the forest wilts. It smells so horribly of rot. I reek so wretchedly of rot.

"What...did you...? What is happening to me?"

You stand unsullied in a barrier of light, crying softly. "I had to, dearest Luminíl. For the good of Harmony."

I retch, pull my knees to my chest and spew agony across dead grass. "What...what...?"

———

BLOOD POOLED BENEATH MIRKVAHÍL, streamed from myriad punctures in her flesh, from the corners of her mouth. "G...Gods..." she half-whimpered, half-gurgled. "Please..."

Mirkvahíl felt a snap so painful and profound she could not scream.

Luminíl gave a great tug, and from the depths of Mirk-vahíl produced the brilliant, six-winged silhouette that was her truest form—the Phoenix. It screeched desperately, its luminescence waning, devoured by Luminíl's rage.

"You took this from me," Luminíl said. "That evening in the forest. Took my temperance for your own because your energy was running wild. You turned me into this! I became the Vulture when this fate was yours to face. I would have helped you. I would have done anything to keep you safe..."

Luminíl shrieked and drew the mirkúr Phoenix into herself. Her monstrousness dissolved and she was once more a woman cloaked and trembling. She knelt at Mirkvahíl's side. Tears fell freely.

"I should have never loved you," she whimpered. "I should have never..."

She sobbed uncontrollably into Mirkvahíl's bloodied chest.

———

YOU BRING MY UNCONSCIOUS BODY to Banerowos, to Alerion—the *false* Alerion. You erect my prison as I sleep, the pair of you plotting falsities in the name of unity, of utopia. Power is seductive. Fear feeds logic to the wolves, and madness runs amok.

You war with those who would oppose you.

You murder those who learn your lies.

Sonja frees me from my cage. You murder her.

I murder you and thus the cycle starts.

You dream your dreams, you take your names, but that voice inside your head does not relent. Subconsciously you know—you cannot run forever. The guilt will always call you back.

———

LUMINÍL PULLED AWAY FROM MIRKVAHÍL. "You made me this," she whispered. "Because of you I wear a monstrous form, but do you know what? *You* are the only monster here. Sometimes the most beautiful things are the most horrible— and what an eldritch thing you are, Mirkvahíl. What an ugly soul you have."

Luminíl stood. "I do not possess foresight, but my instincts tell me somehow, somewhere, in another life, we two shall meet again. But until then, may your Hell be horrible, and may your guilt devour you from the inside out."

She turned from Mirkvahíl,

strode to the edge of the tower,

and leapt.

11

WHERE THE SUN IS SILENT

Banerowos was dead. Varésh knew in his mind and heart the great city had fallen years ago, but to see it once more for the corpse it was pained him terribly. Little more than snow-dusted black stone, crumbled spires rising like a throng of jagged teeth. Old bones littering the streets, and the agony of yore whispering on the wind.

"Welcome," Varésh whispered, "to a place where the sun is silent."

"A morosely poetic epithet," Alerion said, manifesting at his side.

"One that should have never come to be," Varésh said, bowing his head.

"But it did," Alerion said, "and you must live with that as you must live with many sins. If you buckle underneath the weight of your past, of your atrocities...if you abandon your search for Mirkvahíl then you shame yourself, Varésh Lúm-talé. You shame the dead you have made. Is that what you have come here for?"

"No," Varésh murmured. He took a deep breath, steeling his nerves. "No."

Alerion offered an approving nod.

They walked.

"I cannot help but wonder what horrible surprises await me here," Varésh said. "What else have I forgotten, what else yearns to ravage me from the inside out?"

"If you focus on that," said Alerion, "it will only distract you, and that is dangerous here. You have yet to run across Sonja and the other rusalks, and who knows what else lurks in this corpse of yesteryears?"

Alerion had a point. It had been some time since Varésh had seen Sonja. Should she return with the rest of her damned brethren, Varésh wasn't sure he would be able to hold her off, let alone all them, however many the rusalks numbered.

He hissed at a sharp pain in his ears and it nearly made him double over.

"Are you all right?" Alerion asked.

"*Her song...*" Varésh hissed. "Such pain. I...can feel it, feel *her.*" He pressed himself to straighten up and looked about Banerowos. Its tallest spire still stood sadly, if not proudly in the center. *That* was where he would find Mirkvahíl.

Or whatever thing is mimicking her song. The thought

raised goosepimples on the back of Varésh's neck. Until now he hadn't considered the possibility this song he'd been hearing for some time might not actually be Mirkvahíl but something else. Something...malevolent or vengeful. Luminíl, perhaps.

"The only way to know for certain is to climb," Alerion said.

Varésh nodded.

They pushed on.

———

WHAT HAVE I DONE...?

Trees.

So many trees.

Leering, laughing, knowing.

...Gods, what have I done?

Her heart beats yet. My beloved Luminíl.

Gods...what have I done?

...Shut up. Just shut up!

...Trees. Whispering to me. "What a way to end the world, with false hope in a false god."

They know. They all know.

...But what?

What

do

they

know?

———

Varésh blinked. He stood in the anteroom of the spire, mind swirling, buzzing with a frantic memory that...wasn't his.

"Did...you see that, hear that?" he asked Alerion.

Alerion nodded. "Energy runs amok here. Threads and fragments of the past. The destruction of Banerowos, the conflict between Mirkvahíl and Luminíl left pockets to the illum network open. Illum can, to those who possess the innate talent, provide glimpses into memory, into time itself."

Varésh was aware of illum's capabilities. "That memory..."

"Mirkvahíl's." Alerion's expression softened, saddened. "This tower holds great sorrow."

Varésh didn't need the memories of someone else to tell him that. He had been party to much of what had transpired in this place. So much judgment. So much death. So much arrogance and ignorance.

They ascended, the occasional snap of memory assaulting them, though not enough to disorient Varésh as badly as Mirkvahíl's had. What further bits and pieces of that moment in time would he be witness to? His curiosity came partly from simply wanting to peek into the head of a goddess, but mostly it was born of fear. The fear of seeing what he might have driven Mirkvahíl to. Guilt—

———

Luminíl rages in her cage. This...this is for the best.

Right?

"The guilt will always call you back," she hisses. "No matter what you do, Mirkvahíl, it will always call you back. Hell is a place of one's own making and you've just dug your way into the first circle!"

Tears stream from her eyes, swimming in rivulets through the black cracks in her ashen flesh.

Gods, what have I done?

It was necessary.

You were...compromised. You would have killed them all.

You should still kill them all.

I look at the acolytes. I wonder

if they know

how absolutely sane I am.

Stop it!

I had to ...

alter memories...

Everyone...

Rewrite history...

I had to

take

my Luminíl.

Her form.

Her power.

Had

to...

Dying.

...am the Vulture.

Always.

———

VARÉSH SAT FOR A TIME, dazed. Horrified, even.

"Did you know?" he asked Alerion.

Alerion shook his head. Varésh had never seen the Raven god shocked but there he was, wide-eyed and trembling. Trembling still, an hour or so after the memory had left them.

"I...don't understand," Varésh said, trying to comprehend the madness he'd been witness to. "Mirkvahíl is...—*was?*—the true Vulture goddess, and Luminíl was the Phoenix?" He massaged his forehead, then rubbed the space between his eyes.

"It should have been Mirkvahíl inside the cage," Alerion said. *"For so many reasons."*

His form dissolved, leaving Varésh to his own devices in the ruined spire.

Am I to blame for this? He had no recollection, had seen nothing to suggest he had swayed Mirkvahíl to such an atrocity, not that he was anyone to judge.

He pressed on, finally emerging from the darkness, greeted by a cold, gray sky and a figure curled into a ball.

"Mirkvahíl." Varésh was certain of it.

Despite being—no, *masquerading* as the embodiment of preservation, renewal, and creation, Mirkvahíl looked closer to death than rebirth. What had happened to her? How long had she been here?

"Hell is a place of our own making," Mirkvahíl murmured.

"I know."

Her eyes were the darkest shade of black Varésh had ever seen. He studied her, gazed past the sorrow and ruin, and realized

She is Rhona, which means Luminíl is Djen. It made sense in the way a parable should, especially given what piece of Mirkvahíl's dream Alerion had shown him several nights ago. Her conversation with Varésh in his home.

Mirkvahíl gripped his arm and pulled herself upright. "Hell is a place of lies, a thing we dream to escape our deepest fear. But the truth is never far behind; the guilt will always call us back."

She looked at Varésh, tears streaming down her cheeks. Did she recognize him as the lie he was or did she think him Alerion?

"I should never have... I should have died. It should have been absolute. My Luminíl..."

Varésh knew how that felt. He had condemned Sonja to her end. Gods, what a pair he and Mirkvahíl were. Two vultures playing at gods. What a way to end the world, with false hope in false gods...

"I wish I had stayed dead," Mirkvahíl said. "It would be the very least I deserve. So much death...on my hands." She coughed, spitting blood. "I wish...I wish I would stay dead this time."

Varésh took her hands in his. "*Our* hands, Mirkvahíl." He paused. "But we are here, and...there is a chance to set things right, but it will not be easy by any means."

"What do...you mean?"

He cradled the false Phoenix in his lap. She was beginning to fade, her body turning to ash. "Luminíl runs wild. Her entropic power is unbounded by our doing and I know not whether she is in control of the mirkúr; she may be a slave to herself. For now the best thing we can do is temper the entropy, keep it from wholly devouring Harthe."

Mirkvahíl groaned. "And how will you—we—do that...?"

"The past informs the present. I have begun to sow the seeds," Varésh said. "In a place far from this ruin and decay. They are an incipient race, but in time they will help us right our wrongs. They will help us reshape Harthe. Will you help me, Mirkvahíl? Will you take this chance at reclamation with me?"

She was silent a while. As the minutes passed, as she waned, Varésh was increasingly sure she would leave him without an answer. But she did not.

"Without preservation, entropy erodes," murmured Mirkvahíl. "A...world will only survive...if there is balance." She looked Varésh in the eyes and it was like being addressed by a gathering storm. "We will rebuild. We will rectify. We will reshape. But for now..."

She closed her eyes. "With every life, another name. With every life, a memory...entombed."

Mirkvahíl fell to ash, leaving only a brilliant white-gold feather in her wake. Varésh took it lightly in his hand, gazing out across the ruin they had made. "Who," he wondered of the false Phoenix, "will you be when next we meet?"

When would they meet?

Varésh heaved a sigh.

Snow fell,

and the world

was

still.

ACKNOWLEDGMENTS

This was not an easy book to write. Regardless of its length, *The World Maker Parable* was a constant source of frustration early on. I had the idea, but I was struggling to bring it to fruition. I did, eventually. I'm very proud of this story, and I'm extremely grateful for the friends who helped me see this book to completion.

Clayton Snyder, Angela Boord, Krystle Matar, Justine Bergman, & Nick Borrelli, I applaud and thank you for keeping me relatively sane.

Angela and Krystle, thank you both for beta reading this story and providing me with fantastic feedback. You both helped me make this book better.

Thank you to my wife, Jenny, and our little girls, Celia and Naomi, to whom this book is dedicated. You make me a better person every day.

Lastly, thank you to anyone who reads this book. You make writing these weird stories worth it.

————

If you enjoyed THE WORLD MAKER PARABLE please consider leaving a review on Goodreads and Amazon. Thank you so much!

PREVIEW
THE WORLD BREAKER REQUIEM

Prologue

I am timeless, though my soul has felt the wax and wane of myriad millennia as I watch realities rise and fall.

The stars shine high above my Rach Na'Schuul as they have done for years; memories and hopes, for my beloved home is dead, cast to ruin by the god-things of Jémoon. By the madness of the god-things by whom I and all my corpse-kin were designed.

The stars shine high above my Rach Na'Schuul as they have done for years, for like this ruin they are slaves to perpetuity. They call these Pockets of eternity Arcadia—but idylls they are not, for what is peace when I sleep circled by the dead, my Listener brethren of yore?

I shan't abandon Rach Na'Schuul; I can't abandon Rach Na'Schuul for I am bound to ruin by a quietus the hands of time would surely gift me if I did.

I sit, now, in the courtyard of a spire-keep and do as I have done for years—

I Listen. To a prelude long and dark.

A herald to a symphony of broken dreams.

Chapter One
Hounds

Avaria Norrith was dead. Or dreaming. For how else could he have come here to this meadow with its silver trees and ocean-colored grass? He looked down at Geph, his faithful longhound, and the creature simply shrugged.

"Have you considered that you might be stoned beyond all comprehension?" Geph inquired. He did that a lot. Talking. Most longhounds retained some manner of silence even after they had learned to speak but Geph was the chatty exception. "Avaria?"

"You know I don't partake," Avaria said, starting slowly through the grass.

"Then why the hell am I talking?" the longhound asked.

"It's what you do."

"Well if *you're* dead," Geph said, "then why am I here? Am I dead too?"

"Maybe?"

The longhound heaved a sigh that fell into a yawn. "Fuck it all, Avaria, what have you gotten us into this time?"

Avaria glared at the dog.

"I'm just saying."

"If you're talking about the time we were interned for defacing Virtuoso Khora's effigy," Avaria said, "let me please remind you it was *you* who climbed atop and took a massive, runny—"

"I was *drunk*," the longhound grumbled. "And the statue called my mother a bitch. What would you have done?"

Avaria rolled his eyes. "The effigies are incapable of speech, Geph. And your mother is a bitch. It's the proper term for a female dog."

"You keep saying that," Geph said, "and every time I believe you less."

Avaria shrugged. "Not my concern."

"It should be." Geph let out a hacking cough. "Where do you suppose we are?"

"If I were to venture a guess? The In Between," Avaria said.

"Then where the hell is Equilibrium? I have a question."

"I can guarantee you, Geph, that Equilibrium remains incapable of manifesting you a jar of peanutbutter," said Avaria, much to the longhound's dismay. "Though I'm sure he'll oblige you with an ear scratch."

Geph gave a houndly grin.

They walked.

"It all feels the same," said Geph. "Have we actually gotten anywhere?"

"Not yet," said Avaria. He had come to this place enough to know the straightforward path was never as apparent as it seemed. "But we will."

You won't.

Avaria started at the words.

Geph cocked an eyebrow. "Are you all right?"

"You didn't hear that?" Avaria asked.

Geph tilted his head. "Because I'm a dog I'm supposed to have spectacular hearing, is that it? Well—"

How long have you been on this path, Avaria? How many years now? Days, weeks, and months spent trying to win the affections of a woman who could give two shits about you, hmm? And she had the gall to call herself your mother!

Avaria whipped around but there was no one there.

Search, but you'll not find me in the grass, hissed the voice. *I'm where I've always been—here, inside your head. Comfy, cozy in this prison that you've built. No—that your mother built. If she had loved you where would you be now?*

A howl erupted from Avaria. The meadow fell to ash, and from its ruin rose a silhouette of smoke and flame.

"*I told you all those years ago,*" the figure said, "*that she would set me free.*" It beckoned with an upturned palm and Geph obeyed, each step leaving gossamer threads of smoke. "*Faithful as always.*"

Geph grinned at Avaria, eyes glowing white, teeth like needles dripping blood.

Avaria retreated several steps. The figure and the hound advanced.

"You'll not escape, Avaria," the figure said.

Avaria turned.

"For I am legion here inside your head."

Sputtered, looking at the blade protruding from his chest.

"And there is nowhere you can hide that I can't find."

Crying now. He tasted blood and tears.

"For then what kind of vulture would I be?"

Darkness.

It was cold this night as Avaria walked the streets of Helveden, Geph beside him as he always was. His brow was slick with sweat and his head stung something fierce. He'd had the dream again, stoked by vultures of his own design.

"Was it Wrath or Envy in the grass this time?" inquired Geph.

"Some amalgamation of the two," Avaria said, fingering his chest. It was tender to the touch; he winced.

"Theories?"

"An answer," said Avaria. "The Virtuosos passed on me again the other night."

Geph nudged Avaria with his nose.

"Honestly...why'd she put me here if I'm never going to leave?"

"Your mother wants what's best for you, Avaria," said Geph.

"She's got a strange way of showing it," Avaria snapped. "Shoving me off to apprentice while Avaness and Maryn took up arms and went to war for Ariath. I've been here half my life, a slave to erudition and abused by my own mind while they found glory in the heat of war. While they made mother proud."

"And you think swinging arms is all that draws your mother's praise?" Geph asked. "You think to her that mastering a blade is the be-all and end-all to life?"

Avaria scoffed. "In Ariath? Yes."

"I think you focus too much on the glory of war," said Geph. "Look around, Avaria. War destroys physically and mentally. Helveden stands half-erect, awaiting its resurrection by the Lightweavers who have drunk themselves into uselessness. The thought of facing vultures breeds fear, and that fear instills the urge to drink. It festers even now, an indomitable infection that has all but smothered Helveden's glow. Is that what you really want of yourself? To go off and come back like...that?"

"If it would make her proud..."

Geph sighed. "Oh, Avaria..."

They walked the rest of the way to the Bastion in silence, Geph stopping to sniff the occasional tree and Avaria brooding all the while. He fingered the summons in his coat pocket as they crossed the courtyard. What could the queen possibly need of him this late?

A frowning stewardess awaited their arrival. "You're an hour late."

Avaria shrugged. "I got lost along the way."

Geph nudged him firmly in the leg with his nose.

"Fine," Avaria sighed. "I was drunk in bed and dreaming of the end."

The stewardess rolled her eyes disgustedly. "Follow me."

She led them through the Bastion, glorious in its whites and reds and various depictions of the raven god to whom they all implored. It was paradise where the Hall of Light-weavers was eternal hell.

Further and further they went. The walls, ceiling, and floor fell to a deep red. Avaria had never been to this part of the Bastion before, which was saying a lot. As a child he'd wandered where his legs and the Bastion staff would allow.

They came to a circular stark white door inlaid with various glyphs and grooves. The stewardess extended a glowing index finger and traced the innermost glyph. Illumination swam through the grooves and into the outlying glyphs. The door dilated, revealing the chamber beyond. The stewardess dragged him inside. Geph stayed put.

Avaria eyed three women sitting at the far end of the room. *Shit.*

"Ah. We were wondering if and when you might arrive," said Virtuoso Khal.

"I was not so confident as Virtuoso Khal and Queen Ahnil," said Norema Sel, the shortest of the three. She dismissed the stewardess with a nod, leaving Avaria to the wolves.

Wolf, really.

He eyed the queen. "Hello, mother."

Avaria stared at the queen. He hadn't seen her in at least a half dozen years. She looked older in the eyes though no less hawkish and intimidating. Reluctantly, if not slightly mockingly, he touched his right hand to his left shoulder in the formal salute.

"How may I be of service?"

Norema Sel gestured to an open chair at the table. "Sit."

Avaria gave her a prolonged stare before accommodating her request. He hadn't seen *her* in a while either. His heart fluttered momentarily. They'd been a pair at one time. A secret kept in shadows, for what would people think if they knew General Sel had shared her bed with *him*, the Norrith family castoff?

"Virtuoso Khal says you're developing well," Norema said.

"*Have developed*," his mother said. "You're able to wield mirkúr as I understand it."

"Have been for ages," Avaria said, picking at a loose fingernail.

The queen drew her lips to a thin line.

"You say that with such nonchalance, Avaria, that it suggests ignorance on your part," Norema said. "There are very few left who can do what you do, let alone as an apprentice."

Avaria considered her words. "It isn't ignorance Nor —General. I'm simply indifferent. What does it matter if I'm able to wield The Raven's Wings? Mastering illum and mirkúr has gotten me nowhere. I'm almost thirty years of age and the Hall sees fit to keep me there until I die."

An exaggeration, but it often times felt like he would never leave.

"I can understand you feeling that way," said Virtuoso Khal. She offered a sympathetic nod. "Apprenticeships at the Hall are notoriously demanding, but they can ill afford to be otherwise." She passed him a slip of parchment. "We have need of you, Avaria."

"It's time for you to spread your wings, so to speak," Norema said.

Avaria scanned the parchment. His eyes went wide.

"A simple yes will do," his mother said.

Avaria looked at the women. "I—"

"Unless you aren't up to it," Norema said. There was a glint in her red eyes.

Avaria slipped the parchment into his pocket. "Of course I am."

"Excellent." Norema gestured toward the door. "We'll be in touch."

Avaria stood and gave the formal salute. Then he withdrew.

"You haven't said a word since we left the Bastion," Geph said.

Avaria nodded. He was prone to withdrawing into himself in times of stress.

"Avaria?" Geph poked him in the leg with his nose. "What is it?"

"Have you heard of The Raven's Rage?" Avaria asked.

"In passing," Geph said. "What of it?"

"They, um..." Avaria swallowed. "They want me to forge it."

Geph yelped. "A weapon? *That* weapon? Why?"

"I don't know."

"Are you going to?" Geph asked.

A light snow fell, dusting Avaria's hair and shoulders as he walked. "Maybe."

Geph whined. "You told them you would. I know you did, Avaria. I can smell the truth on you a mile away." He snapped at a snowflake. "It's personal, isn't it? Fuck all, but of course it is. Avaria, your mother—"

"She needs to see!" Avaria snapped. "I need her to see what she saw in Avaness and Maryn. I want to do something she'll be proud of, Geph. I just..." Avaria heaved a sigh into the frosty night. "I want her to want me like she did them."

Geph licked Avaria's hand.

"You head on back to the Hall," Avaria said. "I need some time to think."

AVARIA HAD ALWAYS FOUND solace in the woods, in the trees beneath the sway of night. Unlike Helveden they enfolded him in silence and allowed him peace enough to think. To brood as he was wont to do. To waltz with the monsters of his mind as they made manifest at his side.

"Envy, Pride, and Wrath," Avaria greeted. They followed him as hounds, threads of mirkúr trailing their wake. He made no move to banish them, but held his arms out wide. "What do you think? Should I oblige them, forge this weapon they so *desperately* desire?"

Wrath snarled.

"It *would* make them see," Avaria agreed.

Pride snapped its teeth.

"True. I *am* the utmost of apprentices."

Envy whined.

"Swallow your fear," Avaria hissed. If he were to fail... "I need to be worthy. She needs to see me as more than just a thing she found in the woods. If I were to perish would she care? Would—"

Pride growled. Wrath and Envy bore their teeth-like-knives as a distant-growing-nearer shriek destroyed the forest calm. Avaria formed a thread of mirkúr to a blade; he advanced behind the hounds.

At length the trees fell to ruin, and they entered a glade. At the center stood a shrine; before the shrine there knelt a girl. Avaria and the hounds approached with heed. His mirkúr pulsed with every step; the hounds dripped ichor from their mouths.

"Who are you?" Avaria asked.

The girl turned. Her eyes were dead moons and her flesh was burnt paper; her hair hung in silver strands. She cocked her head.

Avaria held his blade between them. "I asked—"

"We in this moment depart," the girl rasped, "replacing all that we are."

She stood and took a step toward Avaria, dark energy enfolding her from head to toe. Where once her face had been now hung a snow-white shroud; and from her back, six wings of black.

The hounds dissolved in her presence.

Avaria fell to his knees beneath her sway, cold in his bones. What was she?

"Are you going to kill me?"

She approached and pulled him up into a cold embrace, whispering, "Listen to your dreams, for things are never as they seem. We in this moment depart, replacing all that we are..."

She was gone, and Avaria was holding mist.

ABOUT THE AUTHOR

Fantasy Author. Long Doggo Enthusiast. Snoot Booper. Shouter of Profanities. Drinker of Whiskey. These are all titles. Luke is the Khaleesi nobody wanted and the one they certainly didn't deserve, but here we are, friendos... He lives in Pasadena, California with his wife and their twin daughters. Somehow, they tolerate him.

Printed in Great Britain
by Amazon

68613623R00095